COMMENTS ON L.C. HAYDEN'S WRITING

WHO'S SUSAN?

Here's one hot mystery story with a child in jeopardy, amnesia, a chase in the Southwestern desert. It's a novel with real people in real trouble. Highly recommended. *New Mystery Magazine*

This suspense has twists and turns that keep you guessing. I loved Detective Bronson, just like a bulldog, he won't let. *Virginia Kachelmeier, The Monitor*

WHEN COLETTE DIED

This is fine example of a women-in-jeopardy novel. The heroine is appealing and vulnerable, the hero handsome and brooding and the situation fraught with menace. This is a fun book to kick with and enjoy. *Toby Bromberg Romantic Times*

Hayden's character development is skillful and intriguing. The plot is fast-paced and generally engrossing. *S. Derrickson Moore, Sun-News*

WHERE SECRETS LIE

WHERE SECRETS LIE is an absorbing suspense novel, filled with red herrings, that will have you dashing down many wrong turns in your efforts to solve the puzzle. She brings such depth to her characters that you sometimes forget they aren't real. This is a good old-fashioned heroine in danger suspense novel that will keep you on the edge of your seat until the very last page. *Kathy Thomason, The Butler County Post*

WHEN ANGELS TOUCH YOU

Inspiring, heartwarming, tear jerking—this book left me spiritually uplifted, renewed my faith, and gave me confidence in the power of miracles....*Kate Wiederkehr, Texas A&M*

WHAT OTHERS KNOW

What Others Know

By

L.C. Hayden

Top Publications, Ltd.
Dallas, Texas

If friends make the world richer, then I'm the richest person alive. Thanks for your friendship and love.

To the Wiederkehrs In El Paso:
Alex and Marie

In College Station:
Kate Wiederkehr

and

To the Wickes in Alaska:
Bruce, Jennifer, and Melissa

Also,
In loving memory, to Linda Burnham

Acknowledgments

A book is never the result of a single author's efforts, but the accumulation of many people's expertise. This book is no exception. Consequently, there's a ton-and-a-half of people I'd like to thank. First, there's my critique group whose suggestions helped to shape and mold this work. Susan Streib, Charlene Tess, Lee Taylor, and Rich Hayden—my hat goes off to you. Thanks a ton!

Then there's the group of folks who honored me by requesting to be a character in my book: Barbara Bloomer, Pam Banis, Sylvia Ulan, Loyce Guthrie, Bobbye Johnson, Lisa Littau, Cosmo Grajeda, Marcos Sandoval, Anthony Sanchez, and a host of students—thanks for the use of your name. Any similarity between the characters and the real person is strictly coincidental. Please visit my website (lchayden.freeservers.com) to see the real people.

Lots of kudos to the Top Publications folks who are really top, and especially to my publisher and friend, Bill Manchee, who had enough faith in me to give me my first break and who continues to believe in me. Also, Bill, thanks for all the wonderful suggestions you made. The story is so much stronger because of you.

And always to my hubby and best friend whom without his loving support, I'd wither and die.

A very special thanks to Officer Letty Olivas, a Crime Scene Technician assigned to the Criminalistics Section. I was lucky enough to bump into her during jury duty. She has taught me lots about police work, and if you spot an error, that's all mine, not hers. Letty, thanks for all of your help.

I would also like to salute the folks at the Las Vegas Public Relation and News Bureau. They provided me with maps and an endless source of information.

Finally, two more groups I'm indebted to—all of my readers and all of my DorothyL friends. You're the reason this book exists. You hold a very special place in my heart. I'd love to hear from you. Please write me at lchayden@lycos.com.

What Other's Know

A Top Publications Paperback

First Edition

Top Publications, Ltd. Co.
12221 Merit Drive, Suite 750
Dallas, Texas 75251

ALL RIGHTS RESERVED
Copyright 2004
L.C. Hayden
ISBN1-929976-26-7
Library of Congress #2003117070

No part of this book may be published or utilized in any form or by any means, electronic or mechanical, including photocopying, recording or information storage and retrieval systems without the express written permission of the publisher.

The characters and events in this novel are fictional and created out of the imagination of the author. Certain real locations and institutions are mentioned, but the characters and events depicted are entirely fictional.

Printed in the United States of America

Chapter 1

Two words described Dan Springer's mission.
Simple.
Perilous.

He must walk into the home of a notorious crime boss and rescue Greg Prickett, alias Young Greg. Dan had no other choice if he ever wanted to see his daughter again. His only regret stemmed from having to drag Marcos along.

Dan looked out the car's window into the bright sun of Las Vegas. He could use some light in his life about now. He drew a deep breath. No use postponing the inevitable. He turned toward the passenger seat. "You ready to go?"

"Yeah. I guess?" Marcos dusted some lint off his light blue polo shirt. "I can't believe I let you talk me into this." He pulled the visor down and studied his reflection in the mirror.

"Don't worry. If I didn't know better, I'd swear you were a blond."

Marcos' hand reached for the wig he wore and patted it. "Yeah? What about the bandage?"

"It's white and it covers most of your face."

"Obviously."

"Then why did you ask?"

"I didn't ask. I just . . ." Marcos once more dusted some lint, this time off his blue jeans.

"Stop worrying. Your part is simple. All you've got to do is pretend you're in pain."

"What do you mean pretend? I am in pain just thinking about what will happen to us if this plan of yours goes sour."

Dan flashed Marcos what he hoped resembled an encouraging smile. "Me, too, buddy. Me, too, but don't fret. It should work just fine."

"*Should work?*" Marcos shook his head and threw his arms up in the air. "Did you have to say *should*?"

"Okay, *will*. Is that better? It will work." Dan grew desperate with the slowpoke in front of him. He pulled around the vintage Volkswagen Beatle. "Drivers who can't keep up with the traffic flow have no business on the freeways."

"He's probably too busy looking at The Strip," Marcos said. "People always tend to slow down in this area."

"Probably so." Dan glanced past the passenger's window and briefly caught sight of the tail end of the famous Las Vegas Strip. During daylight hours, the towering buildings competed for attention, but during the night, these same edifices cried for recognition with their thousands of bright, multi-colored neon lights. But right now they stood only as tall, imposing structures. Nobody in his right mind would slow down for that poor of a view, but why argue? Dan thought.

"What makes you think your plan is going to work?" Marcos adjusted the bandages so he could speak better.

"I've checked and double-checked for glitches and am as prepared as I'll ever be." He smiled, nodded, and wished he could feel as confident as he hoped he sounded. He stepped on the accelerator and pushed the forest-green Honda CRV five miles past the speed limit. The last thing he needed was for a policeman to stop him. Yet, the anxiety to get this over with gnawed at him. His insides tightened when he spotted his exit sign.

For the last couple of nights, Dan had driven this route and memorized every curb, every light, and every stop sign beyond the freeway. He knew which cars should be there and which ones didn't belong. Now, as he drove the route for the last time, every muscle, every nerve ending, focused on his surroundings.

He noticed two new cars, but both were empty and offered no threat. Still, he made mental notes and kept on driving at a slower speed. No one seemed to notice him.

He executed a right turn, and Bloomer Palace, as the Las Vegas residents called it, filled his entire windshield.

"Man, that's one hell of a house." Marcos let out a whistle. "I heard it covers three city blocks, but it seems even larger than that."

"Mmhm." Dan focused on the task at hand. He turned into the driveway that led to an iron fence covered with ivy. Beyond it, the vast, well-groomed lawn contrasted with the surrounding desert flora. He rolled down the window and smiled at the approaching guard, a youth probably in his early twenties. He had broad shoulders with bulging biceps and a narrow waist. What he lacked in age, Dan figured he compensated with physical strength, and if that weren't enough, the concealed weapon he probably carried would serve its purpose.

Dan smiled. "I'm here to see Mr. Bloomer. He's expecting me. I'm—"

"Dan Springer," the guard said. "From *Star World Magazine*. That much I know." He looked at Marcos. "Who's the medical case?"

"Marcos Sandoval, my photographer."

The guard pointed to his list. "Doesn't say nothing here about a bloody photographer."

"I'm here to do a story on Mr. Bloomer's new restaurant. We always like a few pictures to go with the story."

The young man's eyes narrowed as he looked at Marcos. Dan tapped the steering wheel impatiently.

"Look, call Bloomer if that's what you need to do—just hurry. I'm working against a deadline."

"Mr. Bloomer doesn't like being disturbed unnecessarily."

Dan nodded. "That's what I've been told."

"What happened to him?" The guard pointed at Marcos. "Why is he bandaged?"

"He just got out of the hospital—bad car wreck. He's in terrible pain from cracking his jaw on the steering wheel. They wired his jaw shut. He can't talk—but he can still take pictures, so let us in or get Bloomer on the line. Your choice. Otherwise, I'll have to find another restaurant to feature this week."

The guard frowned. "No. No. Don't do that. I'll let you in. I'm just trying to do my job here, okay?" He opened the gate.

Dan waved and followed the long, sweeping driveway. "We're in."

Marcos slumped in his seat. "Wonderful."

Dan focused his attention on the two-story, red-bricked, and white-pillared structure looming before him. It reminded him of a house straight out of *Gone With the Wind*. He had expected the design to be either Spanish or modern, but Bloomer never did the expected. Why would his home be different?

Dan admired the imitation southern plantation mansion that attempted to intimidate by its size. Only the rich, the powerful, and the famous passed through its portals. The field slaves, the group to which he belonged, could only watch from the outside with awe and envy.

Apprehension tightened around his chest as he rang the bell and waited. A matronly dark-skinned woman answered the door. She wore a simple, solid brown dress that made her seem more of a guest than an employee. Other than the gold loops on her ears, she wore no jewelry.

"I'm Dan Springer from *Star World Magazine*." He nodded over his shoulder. "This is my photographer, Marcos Sandoval. Mr. Bloomer is expecting us." He handed her a business card.

She accepted it without looking at it, stepped back and opened the door wider. "Follow me." She led them to the corridor straight ahead of them, under the split staircase. She pointed to the closed door to their right, and motioned them in. "Wait here."

The study, like the rest of the mansion, reeked with elegance. Two walls housed bookcases floor to ceiling. Centered against the wall facing the door, a massive fireplace competed for attention. Above its mantle hung an original Vincent van Gogh he recognized from an article he had written. The name of the painting, however, eluded him. Leather chairs, strategically placed, invited the visitor to come in and read one of the many leather-bound books.

Marcos set the large camera case on the coffee table and flopped down on a leather chair by the fireplace. Dan sat across from him on the couch. A few seconds later a petite brunette stepped in. She wore a tight red jumpsuit that revealed every curve she had. Dan recalled how a recent gossip column mentioned that every Las Vegas showgirl envied those curves. He had thought that to be an exaggeration. Now he agreed.

She wore her collar up, adding a touch of elegance to her regal posture.

Dan rose.

"Hi, I'm Barbara Bloomer. You must be Dan Springer." She eyed Marcos.

"Yes." Dan offered her his hand. "This is my photographer, Marcos Sandoval." Dan opened the camera bag and handed Marcos a 35mm camera with a wide-angle lens.

Marcos took the camera and held it awkwardly.

"You must excuse him. He rear-ended someone—didn't have his seat belt on, and took it on the chin. The doctor wired his jaw shut. Unfortunately, he was the only photographer available when I left this morning. He can't talk, but he can still take pictures, I think. They told me they'd try to send a replacement when one came available." Dan looked at his watch. "Hopefully he'll show up soon."

"Oh, I'm so sorry. I'll go notify the guard to be on the lookout for him. I'll be back in a minute." She walked out.

Dan and Marcos exchanged looks, but neither spoke.

When Barbara returned, she headed toward Marcos. "My sympathies, Mr. Sandoval."

Marcos nodded.

While Barbara studied Marcos, Dan eyed her. The pictures he'd seen of her certainly didn't do her justice. They captured a beautiful face and a great body, but they failed to capture her essence. "We're here to talk to your father about his new restaurant."

"Yes, he told me you'd be coming. He asked me to express his regrets that he won't be here to talk to you."

"He's not here?" Dan asked.

"No. My father wants everything to be authentic Italian, so he flew to Italy. He will be back in a few days."

Dan frowned, hoping to look put out. "Great. There goes my deadline." He directed his gaze at Marcos. "Sorry I dragged you out of your hospital bed."

Marcos shrugged and started to get up.

Barbara signaled for him to sit back down and turned to Dan. "You don't need to talk to my father. The restaurant is my idea, and I'll be running the place."

Dan feigned surprise as the first part of his plan fell into place. While he waited for her to continue, he recalled how his unknown source had assured him Barbara would be easy pickings. "Play your cards right. She'll lead you to Young Greg Prickett. All you've got to do is make sure you talk to her when Bloomer isn't around."

Hoping to bring her into his confidence, Dan smiled. "Well, this is a nice turn of events. You're much better looking than your father."

Barbara smiled as Dan retrieved a small spiral notebook and a tape recorder. "Mind if I use this?"

"Go ahead."

Dan turned on the recorder and leaned back. "I am told that Prado will be like no other restaurant in the world. Can you tell me why?"

Half an hour later, he turned off the tape recorder and put the spiral notebook and pen away. The easy part had come to an end.

Part two of his plan would be much more perilous. One misstep could also lead to his and Marcos's deaths.

Chapter 2

Dan briefly scanned his notes before returning the small, spiral notebook to his shirt pocket. "I'd like a recipe, preferably something not too complicated so I can make it myself."

Barbara didn't smile. "I figured you'd ask for one, so I've got one all ready for you." She reached for the index card on the end table next to the plush chair she occupied. She handed it to Dan.

As Dan read it, he nodded approvingly several times. Truth was, if someone had asked him to name one ingredient without looking at the card, Dan couldn't have done it. In fact, he couldn't even say what the recipe was all about. All the words blended together and all he could think about centered on rescuing Young Greg Prickett. "This sounds delicious." He placed the index card inside his shirt pocket.

Barbara stood up. "Is there anything else?"

"Yes. Pictures." He tried not to stare at her body, a task he found almost impossible. "My buddy here gave me all sorts of instructions about the kind of pictures he wants to take." He flipped open his notebook once again. "One of the most important things in his mind is the proper setting. He wants the first set taken in the original kitchen where you first conceived the idea."

Barbara bit her lip. "By original kitchen, you mean the one in the guesthouse as opposed to the one in the restaurant."

"That's correct."

"But why? This one doesn't have the grandeur of the one on The Strip. And the article is about the restaurant."

The way she arched her eyebrows indicated suspicion and Dan felt his muscles tense. "But like you said, the idea originated in the guesthouse kitchen. That's a great human-interest angle." When her shoulders relaxed, he said a silent thank you.

A pause, then, "Yeah, okay." She headed for the door. "I can see that. Come on."

He and Marcos followed her to a structure behind the Bloomer Palace, a place once frequented by top diplomats and movie stars and often featured in the newspapers' society pages. But not today, for this guesthouse, according to his source, served as Young Greg's prison.

Dan hastened his step and he forced his eyes away from Barbara's swaying hips. Focus, he told himself, but his gaze remained riveted on her hips.

Unlike the plantation style mansion they had just left, the guesthouse combined rustic and modern designs, but similar to Bloomer Palace, this other house also stood tall and stately. Its exterior consisted of blond wooden logs that oozed with wealth. A pair of light oak doors opened to a large entryway of high ceilings and recessed lights. The archway directly in front of him led to a living room filled with museum-quality furniture consisting of stuffy, richly upholstered couches and antique Georgian tables. The fully equipped entertainment unit and large fireplace completed the picture of elegance.

"The kitchen is this way." Barbara motioned to the right.

Dan stepped aside and let Marcos follow directly behind Barbara. He used Marcos' body to shield him as he inventoried the room. Off to his left, the stairs. He had been told that the second door to the right would lead to Young Greg. As far as he could see, no one guarded the guesthouse.

Once in the kitchen Dan whistled. "Quite a nice place. So colorful and bright." He walked around the freestanding bar that served as a large preparation area. He strolled toward the bay window and past the glass door that led to a private yard. No guards anywhere.

"Stand over here by the counter. I think that'll make a great picture. Maybe you should hold a pot or something." He looked around again and stole a glance past the side window. No one there. Dan breathed easier. He could do this.

He had to do this.

Barbara opened a cabinet and retrieved a casserole dish with a yellow and orange mushroom design. She picked up a ladle and pretended to stir. "How's this?"

"Perfect."

"Ah jagu ugh gr a aka." Marcos wiggled his fingers as though that described what he said.

"What?" Dan asked.

"Ah jagu ugh gr a aka." Marcos pointed to the window.

"Oh the light." Dan headed toward his friend. "You want the light in front of her, not behind her?"

"Eek la gagu mal eh." Marcos shook his hands.

"Calm down." Dan patted him on his shoulder. "Remember what the doctor said. Under no circumstances, no talking." Dan turned to Barbara. "He's such a perfectionist when it comes to shooting pictures."

Marcos pounded on the counter. "Aa. Aga ja la."

"Marcos, stop. You're going to hurt yourself."

"Gala le—" Marcos' eyes popped open and with trembling hands he reached for the bandage covering his jaw. The bandage between his fingers turned red.

"Good God, Marcos. You're bleeding." He turned to Barbara. "The doctor told me what to do in case this happened. Where do you keep your gauze, Hydrogen Peroxide, and cotton?"

"In. . .in the b-bath-th-room." She covered her mouth with her hand.

"Where's the bathroom?"

"There'sss one d-down here, but the d-dressings and ga-gauze are u-up-s-stairs. F-first door to—to the r-right."

"Come on, Marcos." Dan wrapped an arm around him and led him.

"W-will he be. . .a-all right?" Barbara held her hand over her breast.

Lucky hand, Dan thought. "Hope so." Dan led Marcos out the kitchen. "But it could get nasty. It'll also take a bit of time to get him fixed up."

"I. . .I c-can't stand. . .the sight of blood. I. . .I'll wait out. . .side." Barbara ran out the back door.

So much the better. He led his friend, moaning and groaning, up the stairs. As soon as Barbara slammed the door shut, he took two steps at a time.

At the top, he hesitated slightly as he remembered the call that had started it all. "Second door to the right," Dan's informer had told him. "Young Greg will be there, but he'll have a guard. I told you all that I know. The rest is up to you." The phone had gone dead and Dan's hand had lingered on the receiver. Who had been his informer and how trustworthy would this anonymous caller be? Dan hadn't even been able to tell if the caller had been a male or a female. Great investigative reporter he made.

All he had were his gut instincts, and they told him to go with the plan. If nothing else, he had learned to listen to his inner voice. He stared at the closed door as though expecting it to grow fangs. He turned to Marcos. "Let's do it."

His friend nodded and leaned against him. Dan wrapped his arm around him, making it seem as though Marcos relied on him for support. They advanced a few steps and stood in front of the door.

Dan braced himself and without further hesitation threw the door open.

A huge man glared at him through beady eyes. The guard must have been close to seven feet tall and his body had to be as hard as a woodpecker's beak. Dan focused his attention not on this man's strength, but on the gun pointed at his forehead.

The giant cocked the gun.

Chapter 3

The ringing of the phone formed a lump in Debbie's throat. She almost tripped in her rush to pick up the receiver. "Hello?"

"Hey, Colette. I got some publicity shots scheduled for tomorrow at nine. Meet you on the stage around then. How does that sound?"

Despair washed over Debbie. Bill, her director, remained one of the few who still called her by her stage name. Colette had been a well-loved, talented singer. Her life had been cut short at the tender age of twenty-five when a crazed fan shot her while she performed on stage at the Crystal Palace Casino. Five years later, Debbie had been hired to impersonate Colette. What Debbie had thought would be an ideal job soon became a nightmare when Colette's assassin began to stalk Debbie. "Sure, I'll be there."

"Good. Don't forget to see Marie. Have her do your make-up and hair. I want that professional look for those press shots."

"No problem. I'll call her and set it up."

A slight pause followed. "You okay? You don't sound too good."

"I'm perfectly fine. I've been exercising, so I'm a bit out of breath." She surprised herself. When had she learned to lie so well?

"Good. We don't want a repeat of the—what shall I call it?—the adventure you and Dan experienced. Remember, Colette was squeaky-clean and as long as you're impersonating her, you must maintain that same image."

Debbie knew exactly why her director wanted her to do this. Bill, like a host of other people, had loved Colette. If Debbie did anything that would cast the smallest of shadows on Colette's image, that would be enough to bring on Bill's wrath. "Don't worry. I'll keep her image clean. I hope to God that experience I had when you first hired me was a once-in-a-lifetime incident. I'm not an adventurous soul."

"Good to hear that. Talk to you later."

As Debbie hung up, she noticed her hand shaking. Why hadn't Dan phoned? He had promised to call as soon as he freed Young Greg. A glance at her watch told her that should have been fifteen minutes ago.

She'd give him forty-five more minutes as agreed. If she hadn't heard from him by then, she would call the police.

Even if it meant losing her job.

* * *

The giant's eyes told Dan everything. They were murky brown slits that glared with the warmth of a cobra. Instinctively, Dan knew this man would kill them both without hesitating.

Dan flashed him his most charming, disarming smile. "Sure glad you're here." With his head he motioned toward Marcos. "He's getting very heavy. I need help."

The guard's only move consisted of stealing a glance at Marcos before returning his gaze to Dan.

"Aren't you going to help me?" Dan forced his voice to sound desperate--hell, there was no forcing involved. He *was* desperate.

"Talk—real fast." The giant waved the gun menacingly.

"I'm not privy to any of the particulars. All I know is that Bloomer asked me to— well, actually ordered me to—bring him this character. He refused to cooperate, so I roughed him up a little. Bloomer said he didn't care about that as long as I brought him in alive. He also told me to bring him up here."

"Bloomer is out of the country." The guard closed the space between him and Dan.

"Well, he didn't tell me that today. He said it before he left." It took every ounce of self-will not to step away from the monster before him. Luckily, the giant's attention moved to Marcos, and maybe he didn't notice how profusely Dan sweated. He forced his voice to sound forceful, confident. "I've been chasing this bastard for about a week. It took me a while, but I finally got him. Now, are you going to help me get him in there, or do I have to do it myself?" As if it was possible, he took a step toward the giant. Let him feel intimidated.

The giant hesitated and Marcos groaned.

"Oh great!" Dan frowned. "I think he's regaining his strength. Just what I need." Dan supported his friend's weight by wrapping his arms under Marcos' armpits. As far as Dan was concerned, Marcos was taking this acting a bit too far. He must weigh at least a ton-and-a-half.

Marcos groaned once more and slightly raised his head. His eyes rolled in their sockets and his head dropped.

The guard stepped aside. "Make no sudden moves." He kept the gun pointed at Dan.

As Dan dragged Marcos toward the bed, he scanned the room. Young Greg should be here, but no matter which direction he looked, Young Greg was nowhere to be found.

Damn, now what?

I

Chapter 4

While lying on the bed, Marcos shot Dan a look that asked, *Now what?*

Dan wished he had an answer, but dammit, he'd been promised Young Greg was being held prisoner in this room. If that were true, then he had to be somewhere close by. Somewhere, like in the bathroom or inside the closet.

Dan noticed the closed door to his right. The bathroom or the closet? Probably a closet, since that was the only door.

He moved toward it.

He heard the guard behind him clear his throat. Instinctively, Dan knew the giant had raised the gun and once again pointed it at him.

He stopped, but didn't turn around. "The bathroom. I need to use the bathroom."

"Bathroom's down the hall." His neutral tone reminded Dan of a trained killer.

"Thank you." Dan slipped his hand in his pants pocket. Finding the three-inch barrel of a discarded Bic pen posed no problem. That was the only thing he had put there. He felt one end of the tube. It had a fine mesh screen securely held by a rubber band. He turned it around. At its other end, he found the masking tape.

"That's the closet, huh?" *Let him think I'm a little slow. Just a stupid lackey doing the only job he's capable of doing.*

Even as Dan formulated the thought, his fingers worked frantically to remove the tape, all the time being very careful not to let the needle he had placed inside the cylinder fall out. Once he accomplished this, he planned to blow the needle out with enough force that it would embed itself in the giant's neck.

Earlier, it had taken Dan hours to master this simple

trick. Once he had successfully accomplished it, he practiced it one more time. Then once again and again. Over and over until he felt he was an expert at it.

Then he did it once more.

And now he was faced with the same task, but this time no cardboard dummy with a big red X painted on his neck stared back at him. This was the real thing. No room for error this time.

Beads of perspiration formed on Dan's upper lip. He wished he had practiced twenty or even forty more times. "Think maybe there's some rope inside the closet?"

The guard didn't answer, but that didn't bother Dan. He had successfully removed the tape. He concealed the barrel in the palm of his hand and formed a fist. "I was thinking maybe we should tie him."

"No need to." The guard's voice filled with pride. "I'll watch him like I do everyone else. Nobody's ever gotten away from me."

"Whatever you say." Dan turned around. "We never met. I'm Dan Springer and you are?"

The giant stared at him.

"You do have a name, don't you?" Dan withdrew his fist from his pocket, his hand firmly concealing the homemade weapon.

"Cosmo Grajeda." He spat the words out as though revealing the information caused him disdain.

"It's nice to meet you, Cosmo Grajeda." Dan coughed once, followed by a series of hacking grunts. He covered his mouth with his fist and used the motion to place his lips around the top of the barrel.

Dan envisioned the target he had used for practicing purposes. He had perfected his aim until each time he hit the center of the red X. The only difference between that and this was that Cosmo's neck was not marked, but in Dan's mind's eye, he could see the X. He felt ready.

He blew out the needle.

It embedded itself in Cosmo's neck. His eyes popped as wide as saucers and he clawed at his neck. "You son of—." He rushed toward Dan.

A flood of adrenaline pumped through Dan's body. The fast acting sedative was supposed to work instantly. What had gone wrong? Dan braced himself for the attack.

He waited until Cosmo was close enough before hitting him as hard as he could just below the breastbone. The giant whooshed aloud as air expelled from his lungs. The blow caused him to lose his balance, but much to Dan's disappointment, Cosmo soon regained it. He staggered forward.

Dan clasped his hands together with the intention of bringing them down on Cosmo's neck. He didn't need to bother. The sedative had taken effect and the huge man lay sprawled on the floor like a dead laboratory rat.

"Wow!" Marcos sat up. "For a minute there, I thought you were a goner."

"Yeah, me, too, buddy. By the way, thanks for coming to the rescue." Dan could feel his heart pounding hard against his chest, like a herd of galloping horses.

"Hey, what could I do? I was supposed to be unconscious. Remember?"

"You better get conscious real fast and help me find Young Greg. If we can't rescue him, our mission is doomed."

"I'm over here."

Both Dan and Marcos turned toward the source of the voice.

Young Greg slid from under the bed. "Boy, am I glad to see you guys." He gazed at his bodyguard's inert body. "I can't believe you did that. You must lift weights."

"My strength lies in the needle dipped in poison. He'll be sleeping for a couple of hours and when he wakes up, he won't be feeling too good for an hour or so. But in the end, he'll be okay. You're Young Greg Prickett?"

The youth nodded as he dusted himself off. "Did I hear you say you came here to rescue me?"

Dan helped Marcos remove the bandages. They had practiced this step several times and Dan felt like a professional bandage remover. He'd have to keep this in mind and include it in his resume. "That's the plan. Are you okay?"

Young Greg nodded.

Once the bandages were off, Marcos removed his shirt and blond wig. "These are for you." He handed Young Greg the wig and shirt. From his pocket, he retrieved a new roll of bandages.

Young Greg stared at the props with a confused look. "What am I supposed to do with these?"

"It's a disguise." Dan put the wig on Young Greg's head, carefully hiding all traces of his chocolate colored hair. "You're my photographer. Your name is Marcos Sandoval, and you recently were in an auto accident. Your jaw is wired shut. Your doctor told you not to try to talk but you don't follow directors too well, so you started bleeding. I brought you up here, cleaned you up as best as I could, and now I'm taking you straight back to the doctor. You got that?"

"I think so." The youth nodded and slipped the shirt on. It was one size too large.

Dan hoped Barbara wouldn't notice. "Remember. Don't talk. Pretend you're in pain and are ready to pass out. Anybody asks you anything just moan and groan. We better put a move on. Are you ready?"

"I guess so."

"Don't talk, remember? Are you ready?"

"Yeah. Let's get out of here."

"You're talking again."

"Sorry."

Dan stared at him and Young Greg covered his mouth.

"Much better." Dan playfully punched him on his shoulder. "Now, let's do this."

He wrapped his arm around Young Greg and Marcos showed him how to lean on Dan. "That'll make people think you're really weak."

Dan flashed him a forced smile. "Yeah, like you did coming up here. You nearly killed me. You're one heavy bastard. Lose some weight."

"Hey, you're the one who said to act as if I'm one-hundred percent dependent on you."

"Yeah, but you said it, buddy. The word is *act*. I should have dropped you. That's what I should have done."

"What if I hadn't fallen? Then what? Our cover would have—"

"Hey, guys, I thought both of you were here to rescue me."

Dan and Marcos eyed each other. "Kid's right, you know. But don't you think this is over. I'll get you for this." Dan signaled for Young Greg to join him. "Come on, kid, let's go."

"I'm not a kid. In a couple of weeks I'm graduating from high school."

"Great. He's just like you." Dan cast his eyes toward the ceiling.

"What's that supposed to mean?" Marcos asked.

"Guys!"

Both Dan and Marcos gave Young Greg the thumbs-up signal. "Let's do it." Dan wrapped his arm around Young Greg, and the youth leaned into him the way Marcos had shown him.

Dan nodded approvingly. "See how he does it? That's what you should have done."

"Then he's doing it wrong." Marcos looked at Young Greg. "Place all your weight onto Dan. He's a big man. He can handle it."

Young Greg's eyes twinkled as he looked at Marcos. "What about you? How are you going to get out of here?"

Dan waved his hand as though dismissing the subject. "That's the best part of the plan. We're leaving him here."

Marcos flashed him a fake smile. "Very funny." He looked at Young Greg. "We got it worked out. Don't worry. Now get going while we still can."

Dan gave the thumbs up signal again, and he and Young Greg headed down the stairs and out the kitchen door.

Barbara greeted them. "There you are. I was getting worried. I'm sorry I didn't come up and help but I don't do well around blood." She smiled apologetically. "How's he doing?"

"Not that good." Dan gave his friend a sympathetic look. "I'm taking him back to the doctor. You don't mind if we continue this some other day, do you?"

Barbara looked disappointed but forced a smile. "No, of course not. He really shouldn't have come in that condition anyway."

"I know. I'm so sorry. I was really expecting a replacement but no such luck.."

The kitchen door opened and Marcos stepped out. He carried a 35mm camera with a telephoto lens. "Hi," he said.

"Danny boy. There you are," Dan said. "Barbara, this is Daniel Hernandez, one of our other photographers at the *Star World Magazine*." He shook Barbara's hand.

"It's about time you got here," Dan said as he struggled to get "Marcos" in the car.

"Sorry about that. Traffic was heavy, and you know I've been having trouble with the old clunker. It finally broke down about a block from here. I had to walk the rest of the way." He pointed at "Marcos." "What happened to him?"

"He had an accident." Dan closed the car door. "I'm taking him back to the doctor's office. I could use some help. I'll drop you off at your car later on."

"You're the boss." He climbed into the car.

"Wait," Barbara said.

Dan held his breath.

"He left his camera bag in the kitchen."

Dan let out his breath.

Barbara said, "I'll go get it." She ran in and returned in a few minutes.

Dan grabbed the bag and put it on the floor in the front passenger seat. "Thanks."

"When are we going to do the interview?"

"I'll call you later on today and set something up." He got into the car and slowly drove off before Barbara had more time to think. The last thing he needed to do was arouse someone's suspicion.

He had hoped the guard would open the gate when he saw the car approach. Instead, he stood in the middle of the driveway, eyeing Dan.

Something in his look told Dan the guard wasn't going to let them out.

Chapter 5

Dan brought the car to a stop and rolled the window down. He smiled and nodded at the guard.

"You're finished already?" A note of suspicion rang in the guard's voice.

"Nope, we're going to have to come back and finish."

The guard leaned down so he could see inside the car. He looked past Dan. "What happened to him?" He extended his index finger and pointed it at "Marcos."

"Started bleeding. We're on the way to the hospital." Dan hoped the guard would have enough compassion to step back and open the gate. No such luck.

Instead, the guard said, "I see you picked up an extra passenger. How did you manage that?"

"He was with Barbara. We're giving him a ride back to his apartment."

"I wasn't notified about that."

"I'm sure Barbara doesn't report her personal life to you." Dan placed his left hand on the door handle.

The guard eyed him and for a moment Dan felt he was about to let them through.

The gatekeeper rubbed his chin as though considering what to do. "I'll verify your story. You wait here."

Dan shrugged. "Just hurry. My buddy's in real pain."

The guard nodded and started to straighten up. The instant he was distracted, Dan reached out with his extended index and middle fingers and poked him in the eyes.

The surprised man screamed in pain as he reached for his eyes. Dan swung the car door open and slammed it against the guard's stomach. He let out a loud whoosh, as air left his body, and he doubled over in pain.

Dan jumped out of the car, placed himself behind the guard and with his hands clutched together, he brought them down on the back of the man's neck.

Young Greg stuck his head out the window. "Wow! Where did you learn to do that?"

That had been a different time, a different Dan. A detective had taught him how to fight dirty. He had to learn it, if he expected to survive. "Just something I picked up somewhere."

Dan stared at the guard's inert body. When he was sure the man wouldn't get up, Dan bolted toward the gate and swung it open.

Marcos scooted over to the driver's seat and sped through. A few feet past the gate, Marcos brought the car to a screeching halt. Dan jumped in and they sped off.

"I can't believe you told Barbara my name was Daniel Hernandez. Couldn't you come up with something a little more original?"

"What's wrong with that? I'm—"

"You're Dan, not Daniel."

"That's—"

"Hey, both of you Dans or Daniels, whatever you want to call yourselves."

Dan and Marcos turned to look at Young Greg.

"I'm Greg Prickett, or as everyone calls me, Young Greg."

"I'm Dan Springer and this is Marcos Sandoval. Why do they call you Young Greg?"

"I had an Uncle Greg. When people called me, he'd answer, or vise versa. Everyone got tired of that, so they started calling me Young Greg. I guess the name just kinda stuck, although I hate it. Sounds like a little kid." He looked out the window. "I can't believe I'm free. It feels so great. Thank you so much."

"Before you thank us, you may want to find out why we did it." Dan looked out the window, away from Young Greg's puzzled gaze.

Chapter 6

Stephanie Sandoval, a pleasantly plumb woman in her mid-thirties, ran out to greet her husband. She wore a blue turtleneck blouse and blue jean shorts. "Marcos, you're home early. Is everything okay?"

"Of course. Dan and I just finished, uh—" He glanced at Dan who looked everywhere but at him. "—an assignment and he needed the phone so we stopped by."

Stephanie nodded and turned her attention to Dan. She gave him a kiss on the cheek. "Good to see you again. How's Debbie?"

Probably all nerves. He knew he was late in calling her. "She's fine, and speaking of Debbie, I need to call her. Mind if I use your phone?"

For the first time Stephanie noticed the youth sitting in the front passenger seat.

"That's Greg Prickett." Dan signaled for him to join them.

Stephanie brought her arms to her throat like a heroine of a silent movie. "Greg Prickett? The Greg Prickett? The one known as Young Greg?" She lowered her voice. "What's he doing here? What's going on?"

Marcos wrapped his arm around his wife. "There's nothing to fret about. I'm doing Dan a favor. I'll explain later." He turned to Dan. "Go on. Use the phone."

Young Greg joined them. He nodded a hello at Stephanie and followed Dan inside the house.

"I can't believe you guys." Young Greg shook his head.

"Can't believe what?"

"Like this is the twenty-first century, you know. You two are reporters and neither of you has a cell phone. Man, that's like unbelievable."

"Technically, Marcos is a photographer, not a reporter. And yes, we're hip. We're in with modern technology. We both have cell phones. We chose not to bring them."

"Why?"

"If something went wrong . . . if we had been caught . . . those phones would contain a lot of information."

"Oh, right. Good point."

Dan reached for the phone, stopped, and turned toward Young Greg. "Speaking of modern conveniences, does your dad have Caller ID?"

"Doesn't everybody?" the youth answered.

Of course. We're into modern technology. Dan replaced the phone in its cradle. "In that case, let's use the convenience store's phone. It's only a couple of blocks from here."

As they walked past Marcos and Stephanie, Dan said, "His phone's got Caller ID."

Marcos nodded. "Glad you thought about that. I really like my house and family the way they are."

"You are so picky. It's a wonder how I can stand to work with you."

"That's simple." Marcos grinned. "You go for the best."

Dan smiled and patted his friend on the back. "Don't let your head get all swollen or anything like that, but you really are the best. Thanks for what you did. I owe you big time."

"And I won't let you forget."

"That's what I'm afraid of." Dan gave Stephanie a peck on the cheek. "Take care of him." He jumped in the car, dragging Young Greg with him and drove off. Five minutes later, he reached the store.

Dan searched his pockets for the correct change. He dropped the coins in the slots, and dialed Debbie's number.

She picked up on the second ring. "Hello?" She sounded breathless.

"It's me."

Debbie remained silent. He heard her muffled sniffles and he knew she had been crying. Damn. He had never meant to hurt her. He had promised her the world and delivered nothing. "Debbie." The word came out almost as a whisper. I love you. He tried to say it aloud, but the words became a tangle of letters in his throat. "You okay?"

"Me, okay?" She paused. "You're the one out there who is risking his life for . . . for . . . Are you okay?"

"Yes. I've got Young Greg with me. I'm going to meet with his dad now."

"Oh, God, you haven't done that yet?"

"No, but believe me. It's all right. I explained everything to Young Greg, and he's on my side. He's agreed to go along with it."

"Call me when it's over?"

"Of course." The silence that followed tore at his heart. "Debbie, I . . ." *I love you. Say it.* ". . . hope you're okay."

"I'm fine, Dan. I'll wait for your call."

Dan kept the phone plastered to his ear, listening to the dull hum of a disconnected line. His stomach filled with disgust and contempt. He was a despicable man. Debbie deserved better.

Then he thought of his wife, Linda, and their beautiful baby daughter, Diana. Images of bloodstains filled his vision. The coppery-smell of dried blood attacked his nostrils.

Anxiety crept up his esophagus and got stuck in his throat. He couldn't swallow. He couldn't breath. He clenched his fists, and involuntarily, they shook. He handed the phone to Young Greg. "Call your dad," he ordered. He fished into his pocket for the proper change.

"Was that Debbie Gunther, the Colette impersonator, you called?"

Dan couldn't bring himself to answer. He nodded.

"Wow. Are you like going with her?" His saucer size eyes told Dan he was impressed. "She is so beautiful. And I love to hear her sing—and not just when she impersonates Colette but also like when she sings on her own. You know what I mean?"

Dan nodded and dropped the coins in the slots. "Call your dad and tell him I want to talk to him. Tell him to come alone."

Young Greg grabbed the phone. "I'd love to meet her. Think maybe you could arrange that?"

"Sure. Soon as this ordeal is over, we'll do that." Dan rubbed the bridge of his nose.

"Cool." The teen beamed as he dialed the number.

In spite of his anguish, Dan smiled.

Young Greg spoke into the receiver. "Hey, put my dad on, okay?" He paused. "Yeah, sure, I'm okay." Another pause, then, "Hey, Dad. You should have—what?" This was immediately followed by, "I'm okay, Dad—nah. I really am okay—I'm at a public phone somewhere, not quite sure where—Man, you don't understand. I've already been rescued. Sort of. My rescuer is pointing a gun at my forehead." He looked at Dan, winked, and shrugged.

Dan pointed to himself and mouthed the words, "Who, me?"

"Dad, he means business." Young Greg's tone sounded earnest and Dan thought Young Greg was probably involved with the Drama Club in his high school. If not, he was surely taking a creative writing course. Or maybe he had learned all of the BS from his dad. It didn't matter. It worked and that's the important part.

"He wants to speak to you, Dad. Alone. Please don't bring any of your men. Like I said, this dude means business."

A temporary pause followed by the string of curt answers, "I don't know,"—"Yeah, I guess,"—"Very sure."—"Nah, he wants to talk to you in person, not over the phone."—"Dad."—"Dad, listen—"

Dan grabbed the phone away from the teenager. "You want to see your son alive, meet me on the corner of Charleston and Decatur. Just you. No bodyguards." He hung up the phone before Prickett could respond and turned to Greg. "Your part is over. Thanks for your help."

"Thanks for rescuing me. Bloomer would have killed me to get what he wanted."

They reached the car and Dan unlocked it. "And what did he want?"

Young Greg climbed in the car and buckled his seat belt. "He needed to distract my dad. He was muscling in on some of his territory. With me gone, my dad would be too preoccupied to deal with it. Once it was over, I'd be released. Bloomer promised."

"Sounds like you don't believe it." Dan started the engine and pulled out of the parking lot.

"Hell no! I know too much. I was as good as dead."

Dan looked out the rear view mirror to make sure no one was following him. No one was. "Why didn't he kill you right away?"

Young Greg awkwardly shifted positions and shyly looked up at Dan. "If Dad knew I was alive he'd be worrying about me every waking hour. If I was dead he would be tearing the city apart looking for my killer. So once a day, they made me talk to Dad. I was given stolen cell phones. That big dude—what's his name? Cosmo Grajeda?—he held my arm down on top of the table while I made the call. He had a machete and promised to chop off my arm if I so much as gave my dad the slightest hint. I basically read from a script, sending my dad on a wild goose chase." He looked up toward the sky and exhaled through his mouth. "I was scared shitless, man. I really was."

"I'm sorry you had to go through that." Dan patted him on the arm.

"Yeah, me too. Now I see why Brad moved away."

"Brad?"

"Yeah. My older brother. His wife 'n him, they packed up one day and moved. Didn't tell shit to nobody. But my dad, he found out they're in Tucson. They own one of them snowbird campgrounds, you know the kind I mean?"

Dan nodded.

"They've got a kid now. A little boy. And a dog. Never met them. Brad don't know we know where they are." He smiled, but the gesture never reached his eyes.

"Your nephew, how old is he?"

"Don't know. I guess maybe three or four. How old is your daughter?"

Last time he saw her, she was a little over a month. "She'll be seven in two weeks."

"That must be rough on you."

No shit.

"I'm sure my dad can help you. If he wants something, he gets it. Like finding Brad. Found him real fast, but he's never told him he knows. He's forbidden me to contact him. I'd like to see him. Meet my little nephew, his wife. Maybe as soon as I graduate, I can go to Tucson. I heard there's a great university over there."

"I've heard that too. I think Tucson would be a great choice."

"Yeah? You think so? Well, don't tell Dad. He's got this idea that I'll be taking over the family business, but I don't want nothing to do with casinos or gambling."

"Don't blame you. You need to live your own life and the only way you can do that is to get away from your dad and his influences. You're a smart boy. You'll make it on your own."

Young Greg smiled and this time his smile appeared genuine. "Yeah? You think so?" He considered the idea for a moment. "Think maybe I could go to Tucson? I could hook up with my brother and his family."

Dan saw the Meadows Mall and eased into the traffic lane around the parking lot. "That sounds like a great idea."

Young Greg reached for the door handle and stopped. "You know, you remind me a lot of my brother."

Dan thought of his meeting with Prickett and wished the kid would hurry up and get out of the car. "Maybe it's because we've been talking about him. You must miss him."

"Yeah, I do. But you do look like him, not like a twin or anything like that, but like a cousin or a brother. Hey, that would make us brothers. Wouldn't that be something!" He grinned, then went serious. "Listen, man, I'm really thankful for what you've done. I hope my dad can help you find your little girl. I'll do whatever I can to make sure he does."

Dan nodded and felt the world close in on him.

Chapter 7

Dan stopped at the west entrance of the Meadows Mall and let the engine idle. "Don't forget, your dad will pick you up in front of the Cinnabon place in about half-an-hour."

Young Greg flashed Dan a smile that crinkled his cheeks. "I'll be there. Believe me. For once in my life, I'm really anxious to see Dad—just don't tell any of my friends, okay?"

Dan smiled. "Promise."

Young Greg handed him a folded piece of paper. "It's my cell phone number. You never know if you'll need it."

Dan stuffed the piece of paper in his pocket. "Thanks."

"No, thank you." He tapped the car door and walked away.

Dan watched the youth enter the mall before speeding off. By now Prickett should be on the corner of Charleston and Decatur. Dan hoped he would be alone, but he knew better.

A man like Prickett had connections as good as the President himself. Dan wondered if he should be on the lookout for the police. Then again, Prickett was as likely to call on the Mafia. It would be wise to watch out for both sides.

Dan didn't slow down as he approached the designated intersection. He studied the parked cars and the people as much as possible while still concentrating on the heavy traffic. He checked all four corners. Prickett was not there. Damn. Dan drove on down Charleston, past Decatur.

Several blocks ahead, he executed a left turn, went around the block, and headed on down past the intersection again. Still no Prickett. Double damn.

Now what?

He was almost a block away when in the rear view

mirror he saw a limousine pull to the curb. "It figures." Dan watched Prickett step out. The limousine drove away. Dan made a left turn, went around the block, and slowed down as he approached the intersection.

Dan left the engine running and swung the car door open. "Prickett, jump in."

Prickett hesitated, looking first to his left, then to the right.

"Now!"

Prickett stepped in. He glared at Dan.

"I have no plans to harm you or your son." Dan focused his attention on the rear view mirror. Three cars pulled in behind him. Interesting. "Look, I just want to talk to you." One of the cars behind him accelerated, drove past him and switched lanes so that now it was in front of him.

"I'm the only one who knows where your son is. If I were you, I'd call off those goons surrounding us." The car beside him stopped, as did the car in front of him. Dan was trapped.

"I'm not even armed. If you want, we'll step outside. We'll talk out there on the sidewalk." People behind him began to honk. "Five minutes," Dan said. "That's all I want. Just five minutes of your time."

"Park the car." Prickett signaled his men to keep moving. "You got three minutes to convince me why I shouldn't have, as you call them—my goons—beat the shit out of you. I guarantee they're experts in getting information. In the end, you'll be begging to tell us where my son is."

Dan parked the car and stepped out. "Young Greg is at the mall."

Prickett followed him out the car. "I will—" He paused. "What did you say?"

"I said he's at the mall."

"The mall?"

"The Meadows. He's waiting in front of the Cinnabon for you."

Prickett's eyes narrowed as though studying Dan. He retrieved his cell phone, dialed a number, and hissed an order to get his son. The cars that had been blocking the streets moved on and several people glared at them as they sped off.

"Your three minutes begin now," Prickett said.

"My name is Dan Springer and I'm a reporter for *Star World Magazine*." He didn't offer to show Prickett any identification. He figured the best place for his hands was where they could clearly be seen. "My name won't mean anything to you, in case you're trying to figure out who I am."

"You're wasting time. You're down to two minutes." He took out a cigarette, lit it, and blew the smoke into Dan's face.

"Almost seven years ago a young reporter decided he was going to clean up the drug scene in Las Vegas. In spite of threats to his life, he wrote what was to be a series revealing names, facts, and business transactions. When the first article in the series came out he went home and found—" The memory became a stabbing pain in the pit of his stomach. He stopped and cleared his throat. "His, uh, wife had been beaten and shot. She . . . died in his arms. Their one-month old baby was gone.

"The reporter had stood there staring at the empty crib. Wondering. Hurting. Hating himself for what he brought on his family. Then the phone rang. The voice told him to kill the series or his baby would also die. In the background, he heard a baby cry. Then silence." The pain ripped out his insides. "The second part never ran, nor did the rest of the series. Now, almost seven years later, that reporter lives in an unrealistic world. Every little girl he sees, he expects . . . he hopes or wonders if maybe. . ."

Prickett's eyes narrowed as though studying Dan. "You're that reporter, aren't you?"

Dan nodded.

Prickett shrugged as though dismissing the idea. "Touching story, but I didn't take your kid. I had nothing to gain by you killing the drug series. So why are you telling me this?"

"Because you almost lost a son and you must know how I feel."

"Get to the point. What is it that you want?" Prickett took a drag off his cigarette.

"A source, who will remain confidential, told me where your son was. This source also told me everything about where he was being held hostage." Dan paused for effect.

"Go on."

"I took it on myself to rescue your son."

As if on cue, Prickett's phone rang. He snapped it open. "Yes?" A pause later, he added, "He's all right?" He waited for a reply, then he said, "No, just take him home." He shut the phone and studied Dan. "So it looks like you're telling the truth. If you rescued my son like both of you claim, why the charade? Why didn't you simply drive him home? What do you want, a reward?"

"No. I'm not interested in money."

"Then what in the hell do you want?"

"I want information. In return for getting your son back, I want you to use your contacts to find my daughter."

Prickett rolled his eyes. "Tell me, are all reporters as dense as you? I told you before, I had nothing to do with your wife's murder or your baby's disappearance."

"But you have the resources to find out who did."

"Haven't the police and the FBI looked for her?"

"Yes, but all they've come up with are dead ends. You, on the other hand, have sources the police can't touch. I want to tap into those resources."

"Listen, you rescued my son on your own. I didn't ask you to get involved. What made you think I would deal with you anyway? You should have called me when you got the tip and maybe I would have cut a deal with you. Now I owe you shit. You're an idiot."

"Maybe so. But the one thing I know about you is you're a man of honor. I assumed you'd be grateful and would do this simple thing for me."

"That's was mighty presumptuous of you." He dropped his cigarette on the sidewalk and grounded it with his foot. "Still, you're right. You did rescue my son so I owe you something—deal or nor deal. I won't guarantee anything, but I will ask around. That's the best I can do." Prickett raised his hand and immediately a limousine pulled up. As he stepped into the car, he turned to look at Dan. "I will ask around as a courtesy to you for rescuing my son."

Dan tried to hand him a business card, but Prickett didn't even look at it.

"Why would I need that? I know how to reach you."

Chapter 8

Bloomer leaned back in his chair, cast his gaze toward the ceiling fan, and shook his head. The fan provided a cool breeze that normally Bloomer would enjoy. Not today. Rage consumed him. "Cosmo, Cosmo, Cosmo." He frowned and looked toward the giant of a man who sat across from him.

Cosmo sat with his arms folded in front of him, a look of defiance in his eyes. His lips were set into a harsh grin.

Bloomer eyed the rolled up carpet by the bookcase. "How long have you been working for me?"

Cosmo stared at Bloomer but did not answer. He reached out and grabbed the back of the chair. His Adam's apple bobbed.

The two guards posted by the door made a move toward Cosmo, but Bloomer waved them back. Cosmo ignored the guards.

Bloomer stood up, went around his desk and sat on the edge of it, facing Cosmo. He remained quiet and could hear Cosmo's heavy breathing. That son-of-a-bitch was sweating, no matter how cool he tried to act. Good. Let him squirm. "Maybe you forgot how to speak English, or maybe you don't remember. The answer is a hell of a long time, and during all that time, how many times have you let me down?"

"Not once," Cosmo said between clenched teeth.

"That's right. Not once. So why the hell did you chose to do it this time?"

"Not my fault. That bastard tricked me."

"Tricked you? A little reporter tricked a professional like you? What was it you said he had? A blow gun like the ones the Indians use in South America?" Bloomer threw his arms up in the air. "Do you know how incredibly stupid this makes you seem?"

Cosmo glared at him.

"You chose the worst time to fuck up. I'm a dead man, you know that?" Bloomer ran his fingers through his thinning hair. "I'm a dead man."

"Maybe I can convince Prickett you had nothing to do with his son's kidnaping."

"Yeah? You'd do that? You'd take the entire blame just to protect me?" Bloomer smiled at him. "Then *you'd* be the dead man."

"Not if I can convince him I was being blackmailed. I can tell him they were holding my wife. If I didn't cooperate, they would kill her. I was also watching his son, making sure nobody harmed him."

"And who is 'they?'"

"The voices on the phone. You were desperately working to find out who 'they' are."

Bloomer folded his arms in front of him and nodded. "Seems like you've thought this out quite a bit."

For the first time, Cosmo smiled. "Yes, sir, I have, and it'll work."

"Except for one minute detail." Bloomer headed for his chair behind his desk and sat down.

Cosmo's face paled. "Yeah? What's that?"

"Remember I told you, you were a dead man?"

Cosmo's expression hardened. Slowly, he nodded.

"Well, you are." Bloomer opened his top drawer, retrieved a gun, raised it, and pulled the trigger. The bullet entered Cosmo's head right between the eyes.

"Stupid idiot." Bloomer placed the gun in his pocket. "Now the servants have a mess to clean up." He looked at the bodyguards. "Get him out of here. I don't want Barbara coming home and finding him."

The guards unrolled the carpet that had been put there for this purpose, and after several heaves and many groans, they managed to roll Cosmo onto the carpet. With him inside, they re-rolled the carpet. More groans accompanied by under-the-breath curses followed until eventually the guards were able to carry the carpet and body out.

The scene was almost comical and Bloomer would have definitely been amused, but right now, enjoyment was not one of his luxuries. He picked up the phone and punched in Prickett's private number.

"Prickett here."

"Hey, listen, I just heard about your kid."

"Oh, yeah. And what was that?"

Bloomer carefully listened to every word Prickett uttered. Bloomer hoped Prickett's voice would reveal what he was thinking, but Prickett's tone gave nothing away. "I heard Cosmo took him. I had my guards work on him to see why he had done that. I'm afraid they got a bit carried away."

"Cosmo's dead?"

"Yep, and the bad part is that he died without telling us why he did it. I'm real sorry about that."

"Yeah, well, you did good. I knew I could count on you."

"Of course you can. I'm furious he would use my guesthouse to hold your kid hostage. One thing you could say about Cosmo—short on brains but the guy had balls."

"Yeah, you could say that."

The line went dead.

Bloomer kept the phone plastered to his ear, staring at the space where the rolled-up carpet had been.

Chapter 9

"What were Prickett's exact words?" Debbie flopped down on the thickly upholstered couch facing Dan. When Dan had first walked in, she wanted to throw her arms around him and hold him tight. He was safe. Her prayers had been answered.

But something about the way he stood or perhaps the way he held himself clearly said, "Back off." Debbie was familiar with this situation. When she had first met Dan, she could tell he was interested in her, but something kept holding him back. At the beginning, she hadn't known why, and it wasn't until much later that she learned about his wife and daughter. He had been afraid that if he allowed himself to love again, Debbie would be harmed. It had taken her a long time to convince him to let go of his past.

Once he did, a fairy-tale romance flourished. Then for no apparent reason, Dan began to pull back again. And so Debbie had stood at the door, looking at Dan, wanting to hold him, but afraid he'd gently push her aside.

His ice-blue eyes no longer sparkled, but clouded with lost hope. Debbie reached for his hands and squeezed them. "I'm glad you're okay."

"Thanks."

Thanks, not *I had to come back to you*, or *I need you*. *I love you* was too much to hope for. She cast her eyes on the wet bar and mirrors behind it. A half chandelier attached to the mirrors lit up the area and reflected itself back on the mirror. Anyone looking at the chandelier would have thought it was a full light fixture.

Debbie felt like this chandelier. Without Dan, she was only half a person. Anguish gnawed at her as she went through the motions of normal conversation.

"He said that he couldn't guarantee anything, but that he would *check around*, and that was the best he could do." Dan shook his head and slapped the arm of the sofa. "What an ungrateful son-of-a-bitch!"

"But his son did."

Dan's gaze traveled to Debbie's face and his hand relaxed. "You're right. Maybe Prickett doesn't feel he owes me anything, but Young Greg does. He'll help me get to his father." He reached into his pocket and produced a small, wrinkled piece of paper. "He gave me his cell number." Dan's face lit up with the newfound hope.

"Dan, be careful. It's been almost—"

"I know, seven years. Don't you think I know that? The trail is cold. The odds are against me." His eyes snapped shut, and his features tightened like a fist. He opened his eyes and his gaze pierced Debbie's heart. "Oh God, can't you see? Nothing can be right until I know what became of my little girl. One way or the other, I have to know. I'm doing this as much for us as for myself."

Afraid to look Dan in the eye, Debbie focused her attention on the crystal figurine of a dancer centered on the stereo unit. "If you don't find your daughter, will you ever be able to stop punishing yourself? Will there ever be an *us*?"

Dan lowered his head. "I don't know." Abruptly, he stood up. "I best be going."

Debbie nodded. Her eyes focused on the luxurious gray carpet.

* * *

Debbie looked so vulnerable, Dan wanted to rush to her and hold her.

He took a small step and stopped. She was better off without him. He turned and walked out, gently closing the door behind him.

Gently closing the door behind him—Dan recognized the irony behind those words. He had closed the door between them all right, but he hadn't been gentle about it.

The elevator door opened and Dan looked at the closed door that led to Debbie's suite. If he didn't go back now . . . He shook himself and stepped into the elevator. He pressed the button that read *Casino*.

He headed toward the back of the room where a row of poker machines were inlaid into the bar's top. He sat on one of the stools, waiting for the bartender who was busy with another customer. Two bar stools down, a woman smoked her cigarette, sipped her drink, and fed quarters into the bar's poker machine.

The typical casino noises surrounded him. He heard the clanking of coins as they dropped into the bin, each machine's individual song as it lured customers to it, and the constant murmur of voices combined with the occasional shouts of victory or failure.

Most likely failure, Dan thought. *Like me.*

"Hey, welcome back. How you doing? What can I get for you?"

Dan looked at the bartender, a tall, thin man with a Hitler-type mustache. Dan felt surprised that the bartender remembered him. But why shouldn't he? Just about everybody at the Crystal Palace Casino knew him. Not because he was Dan, the great reporter, but because he was the lucky son-of-a-gun who had won the star's heart. "Colette" belonged to him. He had instantly become the envy of everyone.

Yet, he had been nothing but a jerk. He'd done it again tonight. How much more would she endure? He had stretched her love to the limits.

He'd make it up to her, but first he must find his daughter. Of this, he was determined. Prickett's power could guarantee him success.

Tomorrow, he would begin to pull Prickett's strings. Tonight, he would drown in self-pity. "Give me a stiff drink. Anything will do. I don't care."

The bartender wiped the counter around the poker machines. "Uh-oh. One of those days?"

"More like one of those months."

"Yeah? You and Debbie finally split up?"

The abruptness of the words sent a cold arrow through Dan's heart. "What would make you think we're breaking up?"

"I can tell. When you're together, you don't stand close to each other anymore. You always used to have your arms wrapped around each other, or you'd hold hands, or look at each other lustfully. Lately, you look ill at ease together. You know what I mean?"

Dan hadn't realized it had been that obvious. He nodded.

"It's your daughter, huh?"

"In two weeks, she'll be seven." Seven. And he didn't even know what she looked like. Or even if she was alive. "I thought today I'd found a way to find her, but that pretty much fizzled out."

"Tough break, but you've got to move on with your life. You've got a good woman up there waiting for you."

Not anymore. "Where's my drink?"

"Sure you want it? In the condition you're in?"

"You're a bartender. This is a bar. Now where's my friggin drink?"

The bartender slapped the bar countertop and turned.

I'm such a jerk. "Wait. You're right. I don't need a drink." Dan took out a five-dollar bill and placed it on the counter. "What I need to do is find a way to pull some strings."

"Huh?"

"Never mind. Thanks for the advice." He shoved the bill toward the bartender and headed for the elevators but stopped. Debbie was really better off without him. Maybe later, when and if he found his daughter . . .

Tomorrow.

Tomorrow, he'll bring her some flowers. They would prepare a picnic and go to Lake Mead. They'd talk and they would reach some kind of agreement. Tomorrow, or the day after that or the one after that or . . .

As he neared his car, he pulled out the keys, popped the alarm, and slid behind the wheel. He'd use the drive home to think. Plan. Get things set in motion. He pulled out of the parking lot and switched on the radio. Before he knew it, it was time to execute a left turn from Las Vegas Boulevard onto Pecos Road.

Here, in North Las Vegas, the highest concentration of available apartments could be found. He had specifically chosen this neighborhood because of the proximity to his and Linda's former residence. He slowed down and as he approached his apartment unit, something seemed different.

Dan couldn't quite place what had changed, but suddenly his thoughts turned from Debbie to Linda. With slow, deliberate movements, he opened the car door and stepped out.

The same clammy fear that had engulfed him almost seven years ago now wrapped its freezing tentacles around him, smothering him and making him gasp for air. His legs turned to lead. His mind ordered him to go inside his apartment. His instinct warned him to stay away.

Dan gulped down a deep breath and bolted past the driveway and headed toward the front door.

Even before he reached his apartment, he could see the door was ajar, just as it had been that dreadful day almost seven years ago.

Linda had always made sure the door was securely

locked.

Every day, before leaving, Dan double checked to see if he had locked the door.

Yet, both doors were wide open. Then and now.

Dan's heart jumped to his throat. He plastered his back to the wall like he had seen in hundreds of police TV shows and gingerly pushed the door open the rest of the way.

He waited.

Nothing.

He stuck his head in a little bit.

And that's when he saw it.

Chapter 10

Bloomer was no fool.

Sure, Prickett had thanked him for taking care of Cosmo and had tried to make him believe that he was safe.

Bloomer knew better.

That son-of-a-bitch had not believed a single word he told him. Not that Bloomer had expected him to. Still, he had to try. That had been his only chance.

Bloomer realized that he was now a marked man. His best chance for survival meant vanishing from the face of the earth.

At least his daughter should be safe. The code of ethics among the Las Vegas men clearly stated that family members would not be harmed or punished.

Yet Bloomer had broken that code by kidnaping Young Greg. Would Prickett now retaliate by harming Barbara? Should he take her with him?

Bloomer slammed the last suitcase shut and surveyed remaining contents of the bedroom. The huge oak armoire with its door opened contained several suits. The chest of drawers was filled with clothes. He couldn't possibly take them all. At first, he tried to fill his suitcases with his favorite clothes, but the alarm clock by his king-size bed served to remind him that time marched on.

His favorite lamp, the one he had bought his wife for their fifth wedding anniversary, had to be left behind. His favorite pillow, most of his shoes, pictures of Barbara growing up—they all had to stay. Maybe later, he'd get Barbara to bring them to him, or he might even sneak back into Las Vegas and get them himself.

A long, drawn-out sigh escaped him as he eyed the room for the last time. If he made it out of Las Vegas alive, he stood a chance of surviving. So far, two hours and fifty minutes had passed since he had talked to Bloomer—and the clock continued to tick. The longer Bloomer stayed in Las Vegas, the less his chance of survival.

No time for goodbyes.

No time for regrets.

"Let's get the hell out of here," Bloomer told his chauffeur who had already loaded Bloomer's other five suitcases in the limousine and was now waiting for the sixth and final suitcase.

Bloomer walked at a brisk pace toward the car. In the driveway he stopped, turned, and looked back at the house he felt so proud of. He had built it with his sweat and hard work. He had always assumed he would live here the rest of his life. All that effort had been for nothing.

Damn Cosmo!

In front of him, Bloomer's chauffeur waited by the car's open door. Bloomer got in and purposely looked away from the house.

The chauffeur closed the door, got in the car, and started the engine.

The car exploded into a hellish inferno.

Chapter 11

Sweat poured out of every pore of Dan's body. The anger, fear, and anxiety he felt all mixed to form a tight knot in his stomach. He stared at the street, past the apartment's parking lot. All he saw was normal traffic.

He had called the police more than half-an-hour ago. Why hadn't they come? Dan pulled out his cell phone and began to dial. Just as he did, a cruiser pulled up. It figures, he thought. He should have tried calling them fifteen minutes ago. Dan returned the cell phone to his pocket.

A tall, attractive policewoman stepped out. She had a round face and bushy eyebrows. Her short, silver hair made it difficult for Dan to determine her age. Her name tag identified her as S. Ulan. "Are you Dan Springer?"

He nodded and looked behind her. Surely, she hadn't come alone. The back-up units would be arriving any second now.

Her eyes narrowed as though studying him. "Were you hoping for someone else?"

"Truthfully, yes. Not just one else, but several elses. When are they getting here?"

Ulan shook her head. "What city is this?"

"What?"

"What's the name of this city?'

"Las Vegas."

"Right. Las Vegas." She said the name as though the words were crumbling bugs in her mouth. "That means at any given time we're working on two new homicides. There's also an armed robbery in progress, and on top of that, there's a group of disruptive drunks on The Strip. Chances are they're going to turn violent. And that's only the tip of the iceberg.

You reported a simple break-in that happened who knows how long ago. In my book or anyone else's, this doesn't constitute an emergency. So little *moi* is all you get tonight. I hope you're not too disappointed."

"As a matter of fact, I am disappointed. Not because you came, but because you came alone. But I've been a reporter long enough to know how the system works, so I understand about a low priority call like mine, but that doesn't mean I have to like it."

"Agreed, but thank you for understanding." Ulan's features softened. "Shall we start all over again? I'm Officer Sylvia Ulan, and let me assure you that I will do my best to help solve your break-in."

"It may be more than just a break-in."

Sylvia's eyebrow furrowed. "Meaning?"

"It might involve a kidnaping."

Sylvia gasped. "Oh?"

"Come let me show you." He led her toward his apartment. "This is how I found the door, slightly ajar. I pushed the door open, and I saw that lamp lying on the floor."

Sylvia stood in the doorway, looking at the living room. "That's it? An overturned lamp?"

Dan had to admit that sounded rather silly. He nodded.

"So who was kidnaped?"

"My daughter."

"How old is she?"

"Almost seven. She was kidnaped when she was a month old."

Sylvia looked at him long and hard. "I'm not sure I'm following you, but this is beyond me. Have you touched or moved anything?"

"I haven't gone in. Like I said, all I did was push the door open. I used my cell phone to call."

"And speaking of calls, I have one of my own to make. I need to notify the general assignment detectives. You wait here and don't go in. I'll be back in a second."

Great. More waiting. His favorite pastime. Dan flopped down on the stairs. At least the gentle breeze cooled him. Dan hated hot weather. So he chose to live in Las Vegas. Not very smart. But, he had to admit, he loved his work, and that kept him in Las Vegas. He mentally outlined the article he was working on.

Sylvia joined him. "Mind if I sit with you?"

"No, be my guest."

"Tell me about the kidnaping." She took out a small spiral notebook and a pen.

A piercing pain stabbed Dan in the pit of his stomach. No matter how many times he told the story, the anguish he felt surrounded and smothered him. He braced himself and related the almost seven-year old story about coming home and finding the door open. He told her how Linda had died in his arms and how their baby had been kidnaped.

"I'm sorry that happened to you. I can see you're still bothered by it, but you said it happened how long ago?"

"Almost seven years ago."

"And it happened here. In this apartment?"

"No. We had a house then. After Linda died, I hated that house. I sold it and moved here."

Sylvia frowned. "Explain to me how this apparent break-in is related to that kidnaping and homicide."

"That lamp." A wave of panic rose in the pit of Dan's stomach. "When I first entered my house, the first thing I saw was an overturned lamp. I knew then Linda and Diana—" He looked away, embarrassed at the tears he felt ready to erupt. "Today, the first thing I saw when I pushed the door open was that lamp."

"That's it? The lamp?"

Dan looked up at the sky. A few stars were making their first appearance for the night. Some shone brightly. Others were barely visible. That overturned lamp shouted a message to him, and he distinctly heard it. Maybe others couldn't hear it or could only barely make it out. Like the stars. "Yes, the lamp."

"It could have just been a coincidence." Sylvia scribbled a couple of words in her notebook.

"Maybe, maybe not. I believe coincidences need to be checked out."

" You and my uncle."

"Your uncle?"

"Harry Bronson. He's a detective for the Dallas Police Department. He always says, 'coincidences don't just happen. They're, more often than not, the key to solving the crime.' I always try to put myself in his shoes and ask myself, what would Uncle Harry do under these circumstances?" She paused and Dan was sure she was thinking of her Uncle Harry. "I hope that one day I'll be one-tenth the detective he is."

"With a model like that, you can't go wrong."

A red Firebird pulled into the parking lot and two men got out. Sylvia stood up. "That's them."

Dan also stood up and followed Sylvia.

"These are Detectives Andy Scripto and Jesus Gonzalez."

Dan offered them his hand. "Dan Springer." He was about to add, reporter for *Star World Magazine*, but as a general rule, reporters tended to be at the bottom of the policemen's favorite type of people.

"Before we go in, we have a couple of questions for you."

Here we go again. Dan braced himself.

* * *

Dan sat on the steps and continued to mentally work on his article while the detectives performed their duties. Dan watched as Gonzalez bent down and checked the lock on the door, then headed toward the window to his right. Gonzalez said, "This window is locked from the inside and the lock doesn't seem to have been forced open. Who besides you, has a key?"

"The superintendent, I suppose."

"That's it? No girlfriends, no family friends, no next door neighbors?"

Dan had considered offering Debbie the key to his apartment, but he had never gotten around to verbalizing his offer. "No one."

"That's unusual, but I'll take your word for it."

Gee, thanks, officer.

Detective Gonzalez headed around the side of the apartment. "I'll check the other windows, then join Andy and Officer Ulan."

Dan turned away from his apartment and toward the mountains. The back porch of his and Linda's house had offered this same spectacular mountain view. Often, he and Linda had stood and stared in awe at its majesty. Now it looked dark and ominous.

He turned back to face his apartment and briefly wondered how many of the millions of yearly visitors who frequented Las Vegas realized the mountains existed. He could probably count those people on one hand. Pity. People simply didn't look.

That's why the simple detail of the overturned lamp screamed at him. Someone out there boldly told him to ease off. Someone who knew he had aggressively renewed his search for Diana.

Dan glanced at his watch. Ten minutes had passed since the detective went inside his apartment. Unless something drastic had happened, he only had a one-bedroom place. Why were they taking so long?

As if on cue, they stepped out. "As far as I can see, everything else looks normal."

Dan's gaze met Scripto's.

"Are you positive you locked the door? If it was open, neighborhood kids could have come in. They probably didn't mean to do it, but somehow they knocked over the lamp. Maybe they were horsing around. They panicked and left."

True, there were plenty of children in the apartment complex, but somehow he couldn't see them doing something like this. "That's not very likely, is it?"

The detective shrugged and looked away.

"Mind if I go in?"

The detectives stepped aside. "Please do. In fact, if you find anything missing, we would like to know about it. Take your time searching. Call us if you find anything else wrong."

Dan stuffed his hands in his pockets. "This is it, then?"

The detectives nodded and headed to their car. Sylvia hung back.

Dan waited.

Sylvia's attention focused on something behind Dan. Slowly her attention returned to him. "My aunt is probably going to hate me for this. But if I had a child and this child were missing, I..." She smiled, but it didn't reach her eyes.

All the frustration, anger, and bitterness Dan had felt, he could see in her face. "Thank you for coming."

"That's my job. No need for thanks. Now, here's the part my aunt isn't going to be happy about. They're here in Las Vegas for a much-needed vacation. I can call Uncle Harry and set up a meeting. Just to give you advice, mind you. He really does need his rest."

"I'd like that."

"I'll call him tonight."

If Dan felt sure she wouldn't have misinterpret his reaction, he would have kissed her cheek. "Thank you. You're one hell of a good officer."

Her face reddened as she smiled. She turned and left.

Dan stood at the doorway, staring at each item in the living room. The rich, black couch with chrome tables on either side of the davenport, the glass and chrome coffee table in the middle of the small room, the recliner, the TV set and stereo unit—if only these items could talk. He stepped the rest of the way in and gently closed the door behind him.

He would go through the motions of checking to see if anything else had been disturbed or was missing. He knew he'd find everything intact.

The message had been in that overturned lamp.

A warning?

Or a threat?

Chapter 12

The make-up room occupied the right-hand side of the floor level below the stage. The area usually buzzed with excitement and hurried people. Laughter, mingled with an occasional tear, anxiety, and hope, vibrated through its walls.

But not at the early, cheerful hour of seven. After the midnight performances, the sensible entertainers chose to remain in bed. Not that Debbie wasn't sensible. She had, in fact, made her appointment early in the morning so she'd have enough time to enjoy a leisurely breakfast prior to meeting her director.

At 6:55 she dragged herself to her appointment. Why did mornings have to come so early? She swung the door open and stepped into the make-up room.

A woman with a round face and chin-length straight hair bounced to her feet. She dropped the magazine she'd been reading. "Debbie! How good to see you. Gosh, you haven't changed a bit."

Okay. So who was this bundle of energy? A fan, no doubt. A fan who called her Debbie, not Colette. How unique. "Hi, I'm here to—"

"Get your hair done. That's me. I'm doing your hair."

Debbie glanced around the room. "What happened to Marie?"

"Who?" She waved her hand as though dismissing the idea. "Oh, you mean the previous hair dresser? I don't know what happened to her. All I know is that she's not working here anymore, and I've had my name on a waiting list, and I got this call and I couldn't say no. I mean, like I've been waiting for ages to work here and when they called, I immediately said yes. I didn't even give my two-week notice at my previous job. I worked in this little beauty shop on Desert Inn Road. I had lots of customers ask for me and they always tipped me real well, but when I got a call for this job, I didn't care about the other job. This is my dream job, and so here I am, standing right in front of you ready to do your hair."

"Then let's get to it." Debbie followed her new hairdresser to the chair by the sink. "I'm glad you got your dream job. I'm happy for you." Debbie waited until the new hairdresser placed the cape around her before sitting down. "By the way, I'm Debbie Gunther."

"I know. I was waiting to see if you'd remember me, but it doesn't seem like you do. I wasn't going to say anything. I told myself to wait. Wait and see how long it takes Debbie to remember me. I mean like I haven't really changed that much. At least I don't think I have. What do you think? Do you think I've changed?" She wet Debbie's hair. "Now listen to me. How silly of me. You're probably sitting there thinking so who is she? Or maybe now you do remember. So tell me, do you know who I am?"

Debbie ran all the possibilities through her mind. Someone this bubbly who talked this much certainly wouldn't be someone she'd forget. But for the life of her, Debbie couldn't quite place her. Was she someone she'd met in Hollywood before she came here to Las Vegas? Or worse, someone from her life before Hollywood?

The hairdresser massaged Debbie's scalp as she shampooed it. "So you're awfully quiet. Does that mean you can't remember me, or is it that you're thinking of your past and grabbing at straws? If that's what you're doing then you're halfway there. And if you want to consider that a hint well, by all means, you should."

So it was someone from her past. Wonderful.

The hairdresser temporarily stopped massaging Debbie's scalp. "Let's see. I can give you another hint." She squinted as though considering the different choices. "Let's see." She smacked her lips. "Hmm. . ." Her hands rested on Debbie's hair. "I'm really hoping you'll remember me. I've kept up with you, and it would mean so much to me if you'd remember me on your own. I'm a big fan of yours. I was a big fan of yours even before you became the famous Colette impersonator." She resumed shampooing Debbie's hair. "Oh, oh. You tint your hair, don't you?"

"My hair is a darker blond than Colette's hair. As long as I continue to impersonate her, I'll have to continue coloring my hair so it matches Colette's shade."

"No problem. Next time around, I'll bring the stuff to lighten your hair." She massaged Debbie's scalp. "That feel good?"

"Mmhh."

"Good. I want you to relax. That's part of my job. Help you relax, make you beautiful, and continue to make you look like Colette. Now, while you're all relaxed, I want you to think of who I am. Let's see." Pam paused and scratched the upper part of her lip. "I know. I'll give you a little hint, which is not a little hint at all. It's a huge hint. It's my name. But I'll give you only the first name. Then maybe that will trigger your memory. So what do you think? Think it'll work? My name is Pam."

Big help. Debbie didn't remember any Pam's.

"Oh, geesh, you still don't remember me, do you? We'll, I can't say I blame you. Like it's been ages, you know. That's okay that you can't remember. My feelings aren't hurt. But we can pick up where we left off. I'd like for us to be bosom buddies. So what do you say? Would you like to be best friends again?"

Again?

Debbie's never had a real friend in her entire life. Lots of acquaintances though.

"It's Banis. My name is Pam Banis."

How do you do, Pam. The name still doesn't ring a bell. Sorry.

"Do you remember Wiederkehr?"

That's it? One sentence? Debbie had assumed that Pam spoke only in long paragraphs with no periods and commas. Talk about being impressed. "Sure. That's my Alma Mata."

"Yeah. I know." Pam dried Debbie's hair and wrapped it in a towel. "It's mine too. We went to the same elementary school. Remember Mrs. Albert? I still remember when Mrs. Albert…"

That name Debbie did remember. Second grade teacher. Strict, but kind. Probably the best teacher Debbie ever had, until her junior year when her choir teacher Kathy Genes forced her to sing in front of others.

Pam poked her. "What you'd do? Fall asleep? Haven't you been listening to what I said? Gee, if I didn't know better, I'd get my feelings hurt. But I'm made of steel. Yep, that's me. So what did you think?"

Debbie shook her thoughts away. "About Mrs. Albert?"

"Mrs. Albert? Heavens no. That was ages ago. Where have you been? We've been talking about your hair."

"My hair?"

"Yeah. Like I told you. Colette was just about the most beautiful woman who ever lived. She was classy, especially when she wore her hair up in those cute, little, dangling curls. How about we do that? Don't you think Dan will just love it? Imagine, he can put his fingers inside a curl then let it bounce off. Won't that be sensual?"

Debbie held her breath. "Dan…" She felt the anguish choke her. "Dan, uh, won't …be doing that."

"Too shy? You're trying to tell me good ol' heroic Dan is shy? Why I can't imagine—"

The sense of loss left Debbie feeling utterly defeated as though she'd been thrown into a bottomless pit with no hope of escape. Tears clouded her vision and she hoped Pam hadn't seen them. "We broke up last night."

Pam set the trimming scissors down. "Whaaat?"

"It's...best."

"For whom? For you? You look miserable. For him? He needs you more than he's ever needed someone. Now tell me. Why did he break up? Because he's afraid that what happened to his wife will happen to you? He doesn't want to place you in a dangerous position. You know why? Because he loves you. That's why he broke it off. He's willing to be miserable so you can be safe. And are you going to let him do that? No, siree, you're not. Soon as you finish with Bill today, you're going over to Dan's, and you're going to tell him you'll stand by him. You will not let him push you aside." Pam picked up the scissors and continued to trim Debbie's hair.

"How did you know that about Dan?"

"Oh, for Pete's sake, gal. Haven't you been listening? I told you, I've kept up with you, and people around here like to gossip. I listen to the gossip. You'd be surprised how much you can learn by listening to gossip. Then maybe not. Maybe you do know how loose people's tongues can be around here, but back to the original question. What are you going to do about Dan?"

The words to the popular '60's song popped into Debbie's mind. Something about holding him, and kissing him, and loving him. That sounded like great advice. "I actually don't want to lose him. I just don't know if I have the courage to stand up to him."

"Sure, you do. You've always been a survivor. Lack of courage isn't one of your missing traits."

Not according to Grandma. She used to describe Debbie as "an insignificant speck of dust" and "mousy." As a child, as a teen, Debbie, before she became Colette, was timid, withdrawn, awkward. Pam, her childhood bosom buddy, should have known this. "I'm not sure about that."

Pam blew dry Debbie's hair. She used her fingers and a brush to make it go the way she wanted it to. "You survived living with your Grandma, didn't you? Maybe you thought you were oh, so shy, but I thought you showed a lot of courage. Now call on that courage once again and go to Dan. He'll need your strength. And besides, now you can give him a weapon, he's never had before."

"A weapon? What kind of a weapon?"

"Me."

Me? That's it? One word? Now when she should be talking she doesn't? Amazing, this bosom buddy of hers. "Explain." She could play the one word game too.

"Think about it. What do I do for a living? I'm a hairdresser—and not just a hairdresser, but a damn good one. That's why I got this job. Tons of other applications are sitting there but I got the job because I'm so good. Not that I'm bragging. I'm just making a point. Yours isn't the only hair I'm working with. I also do Barbara Bloomer's—that's that woman Dan conned into handing him Young Greg."

Debbie gasped. "How did you know about that?'

"Okay, once more. I'm a hairdresser. People talk to their hairdresser. Late last night, I did Melody Prickett's hair. I do her hair everyday. In case you don't know, that's Young Greg's mom, and she's a talker."

"I can see how you could be very beneficial to Dan's cause. Are you sure you want to do this?"

Pam plugged in the curling iron. "I can always use the extra cash, if you get my drift."

"I'll tell Dan."

And now instead of Dan having to worry only about Debbie's safety, he'd also have to worry about Pam's.

Debbie bit her lip.

Chapter 13

The newspaper headlines read "Bomb Kills Elko Bloomer, Chauffeur." Dan read the article and pushed his coffee aside. Going down, it felt like acid landing in his stomach.

He sat at the Chandelier Café located on the main floor of the Crystal Palace Casino. He glanced at his watch. He had arrived early, fifteen minutes too early to be exact, but he wanted to be sure he wasn't late.

"Sylvia did a pretty good job of describing you."

Dan looked up. He saw a solidly build man with high cheekbones and coarse black hair. He stared at Dan through bushy eyebrows. He wore faded blue jeans and a gray T-shirt. Dan offered him his hand. "You must be Detective Bronson."

"That's me." He shook hands and sat down. "Except it's just Bronson. Real name's Harry, but nobody calls me that. Not even my Carol."

The waitress came by and Dan ordered a Coke while Bronson asked for coffee. "Some people do call me Uncle Harry, though."

Dan couldn't possibly see people calling this block of a man Uncle Harry. "Thank you for coming. I know you're on vacation."

"Aah, no big deal. My little Carol—now there's a woman who loves this place. Loves those Keno machines. Can't get her away from 'em." The waitress arrived with a sweating glass of Coke and a steaming cup of coffee. Bronson picked up three packs of sugar and poured them in. "Don't mind though. That lady is a saint, 'cept for this gamblin' thing. We don't come here often, so it's okay."

"Still, I appreciate your time."

Bronson opened and poured in four tiny tubs of cream. He stirred his coffee and took a big swig. "Aah, nothin' like a good cup of coffee." He retrieved a small spiral notebook, opened it to a blank page, clicked the point out on his pen, and stared at Dan.

Dan sat up straight in his chair, like a schoolboy who had been caught doing something wrong. He said the first thing that popped into his mind. "It's my daughter."

"She has a name?"

"Yes, of course. Diana."

Bronson wrote down her name and looked back up at Dan.

"She was kidnaped."

"Ah."

How was Bronson supposed to help him? He was wasting his time. Dan stirred his Coke with the straw just so he'd have something to do.

"Tell me your story."

"My story?"

"Begin with how you decided to do this drug thing."

Oh, that story. Dan braced himself for yet another painful retelling of the incident that led to his wife's death and his daughter's kidnaping. As he spoke, he felt the familiar fury burn within him.

Bronson never interrupted him. Instead, he took page after page of notes. When Dan stopped talking, Bronson looked up at him. "What made you want to write that drug story?"

He had to be kidding. Hadn't he been listening? "I wanted to live in a clean city that was crime and drug free."

"So you chose Las Vegas?"

Dan smiled. It did seem rather ridiculous. "It's where I live. I wanted my daughter to grow up in a good, healthy environment."

"Don't blame you for that." Bronson finished his coffee and signaled the waitress for a refill. He studied his notes. "You got that first call, warnin' you to back off the story. What'd you do?"

Frustration ate at him. He had already covered the question. What was Bronson doing? Dan answered it anyway.

And he answered the endless repetition of questions that followed. And when he finished, Bronson began all over again. Dan considered leaving, but Officer Sylvia Ulan had been so concerned, he didn't want to be rude to her uncle. Dan braced himself for yet a third retelling.

Halfway through, Dan switched from Coke to water without lemon, thank you.

Bronson continued to drink coffee—three sugars and three creams.

By the time Dan finished answering Bronson's questions for the third and final time, he felt like a hollow man, a robot functioning without emotion.

"Tell me what the police have done to find your daughter."

Dan closed his eyes. No more questions. He answered it.

"What steps have you taken to find your Diana?"

Dan told him everything and finished by telling him about Young Greg. Once again, Bronson furiously scribbled down notes. Dan hoped Bronson wouldn't have him repeat the story again.

He didn't. He told it four times.

When he finished that last time, Bronson studied Dan with such intensity; Dan felt his soul invaded.

"Read an interesting article this mornin'."

Dan felt relieved. No more questions. "Yeah? What's that?" He hadn't even finished the question when he realized exactly which story Bronson alluded to.

"Seems a bomb went off last night."

Dan drank his water and looked across at Bronson. "Elko Bloomer and his chauffeur were killed."

Dan looked down at his water. Most of the ice had melted. He hated warm water.

"Police know about Young Greg and Bloomer?"

Dan shrugged. "You are the police."

"Aha." Bronson scribbled something else down. "So where do you go from here?"

"As selfish as it may seem, my sole purpose of rescuing Young Greg was to solicit Prickett's help."

"Prickett doesn't seem to want to cooperate."

Bronson had to be the master of understatement. "So I noticed. If Prickett doesn't want to help, Young Greg will. He gave me his cell phone number."

"You know you're playin' with fire."

For Diana, he'd dance right into the fire's hottest flames. Dan nodded.

"I admire you for that." Bronson pushed his cup away and closed his notebook.

"I best be goin'." Bronson stood up. "I'll be in touch."

"Ah, yeah. Thanks for your time."

Bronson touched his eyebrow with his index finger as though saluting. "No need to mention it."

Right on. No need at all.

Had the waitress been looking at him, Dan would have ordered a soda and sipped it while he tried to make sense of what Bronson said and tried to formulate some kind of plan. As it turned out, the waitress ignored him. Dan laid a ten-dollar bill on the table, which he figured more than covered Bronson's bottomless coffee and his sodas.

He stood up and stared straight at Debbie.

Chapter 14

Dan hesitated for a few seconds before he approached Debbie. He looked deep into her inquisitive amber eyes, and wished he could read her thoughts. The love he felt for her overwhelmed him and he wrapped his arms around her.

He felt her shaking. He stroked her hair. "I never meant to hurt you. It's just that I'm so afraid that if you stay with me, they'll hurt you like they hurt Linda."

Debbie pulled away from him. Her lips set into a thin line and her eyes narrowed. "You've got to realize we're a team. I'd rather be in danger and stand by your side, than be safe by myself."

She stood with her hands on her hips glaring at him. She looked delicate, but determined. She was his diamond set against a velvety background. He couldn't allow anyone to harm her. "No."

Very slightly, she raised her head and the intensity in her eyes startled him.

In an even voice that came out as a harsh whisper, she said, "You don't have a choice." She smiled and the classical, exquisite features returned. Dan's heart did a flip-flop.

She reached for his hand and led him back to one of the booths. "Besides, I think I got you some help, so you can't turn away from me."

Dan followed her. "What kind of help? . . . Where are we going?"

"I'm thirsty. We're going to get a drink."

That's not exactly what Dan was hoping to get, but it would have to do. They sat down in the same booth he and Bronson had occupied.

"I have a new hairdresser."

For the first time, Dan noticed Debbie's hair. She wore it up with loose curls dangling down. Damn sexy. "Your hair looks very nice."

"Thank you. Do you know who Pam Banis is?"

"Your hairdresser?"

The waitress arrived and Dan ordered a Diet Coke for Debbie and a Coke for himself. The waitress nodded and did a double take when she saw Dan. "You back again, huh?"

If awards were ever handed out for being observant, he'd definitely nominate her. "I guess I'm just in a thirsty mode."

The waitress smiled and left.

"Of course, Pam's my hairdresser, but do you know who she is?"

"The lady who fixed your hair?"

Debbie wrinkled her nose. "Ohhh, you can be so exasperating at times. But you're right. She did fix my hair, but she also fixes Melody Prickett's and Barbara Bloomer's hair."

Dan sat up. "Interesting."

The waitress arrived and set the two sodas down. Debbie immediately reached for hers and sipped it. Dan didn't touch his.

"Women tend to confide in their hairdressers."

Dan wondered what Debbie had told her about him. "And?"

"And for a fee, she's willing to try to extract information from Melody and Barbara. Pam did say that she couldn't of course guarantee results, but that she would certainly try."

Dan considered the possibilities. How reliable was gossip, anyway? "You know I'm going to put pressure on Prickett to provide me with some sources."

Debbie nodded and drank her Diet Coke.

"Do you think Pam could suggest to Melody to put some pressure on Prickett?"

"She can certainly try."

Dan felt the wheels turning inside his head. "What I really want to know is who is my informer. I bet he knows plenty of things that I can use to find Diana. I need to know what others know."

"And you think maybe Pam can help you find your source." Debbie finished her soda and reached for Dan's. "Do you mind?"

"No, go ahead, but it's not a diet."

"Then you'll just have to help me work off the extra calories." Debbie flashed him the type of smile only she could offer. It was a curvature of the lips that spoke of love and warmth and hinted at much more.

Damn sexy smile.

"With pleasure." Dan felt the familiar stirrings of desire form deep within him. He cleared his throat and changed positions. "So you think maybe Pam can dig around, see if she can learn anything?"

"I'm sure she could try."

"Can we trust her?"

Debbie nodded. "I think so. I forgot to mention that Pam and I are school buddies. We went to second grade together, or so she claims. I really don't remember her even though she knew about Grandma."

Hmm, pure luck that she'd show up just when needed. "And you haven't seen her for how long?"

"You know my background. I had no friends. I was a loner. She's the only one who knows about Grandma, but then again, as you pointed out, I haven't seen her for ages. I think we should approach with caution."

"That's the key word."

"Caution?"

"No, approach. Pam wants to either *a*) help, or *b*) she's a set up. Either way, I feel I must play her game." That meant, of course, that Debbie was back in the picture.

Something told Dan that wasn't a very good idea.

He feared for her life.

Chapter 15

Dan kissed Debbie goodbye and cursed his job under his breath. It took all of his will-power not to head to Prickett's. He faced three deadlines, which meant he would probably have to work overtime. Damn.

Traffic today was unusually light for Las Vegas. Normally, driving Las Vegas freeways and streets meant heavy traffic. If he needed to be anywhere at a specific hour, Dan would normally allocate extra time for waiting at endless traffic lights or crawling along like a caterpillar. Much to his delight, he arrived at work twenty minutes early. He could certainly use the time.

In the wee hours of the day, the office was basically deserted with only four or five reporters finishing up the graveyard shift. When it was empty like this, the office looked a lot larger than when it hummed and buzzed with the constant movement and commotion of reporters, photographers, editors, and an assortment of other personnel.

Desks were crammed into every available space, shrinking the appearance of the copy room. The cubicle Dan called his own not only faced the front, but had a side window overlooking the parking lot. How lucky could he get?

He closed the blinds and, as much as possible, turned toward the bare wall. Last week they had been painted beige and nobody had yet gotten around to rehanging their posters, awards, favorite stories, or photographs.

As soon as he had the time, he'd put Debbie's picture back up on the wall. The photograph was one of his favorites, even though Debbie posed as Colette. The poster had originally hung in the entryway of the Crystal Palace Casino. Now, it decorated his office—or at least it did until a week ago.

Right now, all he had was that darn beige wall. Beige, for Pete's sake. Not a color that encouraged creativity. Okay, think. Dan faced a blank computer screen. Nothing came to mind. Let's see, comedy in the Las Vegas shows. Dan didn't particularly feel very funny. Thank God he had already done all of the research and now he faced the task of organizing it all into one neat article. He needed a crisp, attention-grabbing introduction. He glanced at his notes and his fingers flew across the computer keys.

"Lunch time! Let's go!"

Dan abruptly stopped pounding on the computer keys and glanced at his wristwatch. He was surprised to find that over four hours had flown by. He had completed the comedy piece and now focused his attention on the magic of Las Vegas.

"Hey, are you ignoring me on purpose, or are you just ignoring me?"

Dan looked up and saw Marcos standing in front of his desk.

"I invited you to lunch."

"Thanks, but no. I've still got two stories to write."

Marcos let out a whistle. "Two? You lazy son of a bitch."

"Lazy. What are you talking about? I'm working my butt off here."

"I know?"

"I need to keep writing until I get this damn thing done."

"You also need to eat."

"I'll treat myself to a steak tonight."

"In that case, I'm joining you."

"So you think."

"As often as I can. How 'bout if I bring you a sandwich?"

"Ham and cheese. Chips. Soda. Any kind."

"You got it."

Dan handed him a ten-dollar bill.

Marcos looked at it. "It'll take at least a twenty to buy yours and my meal."

Dan placed his hands behind his head, put his feet on top of his desk, and stared at Marcos.

"You owe me, remember?" Marcos said.

Dan retrieved another ten-dollar bill from his wallet and handed it to Marcos. "You drive a hard bargain."

"Always."

* * *

At twenty minutes past four, Marcos approached Dan's desk. "Line one is for you."

Dan waved his hand without looking up. "I'm not doing the phone thing today."

"Except for this call."

"Okay, I give up. Give me a reason why I should pick the phone up."

"It's Prickett."

Dan made a mad dash for the phone, lost his balance, nearly tripped, but caught himself in time. He pressed the flashing button. "Springer here."

"I've got some information you'll find interesting. Come to my house at 8:00 tonight. Don't be late."

So much for the steak dinner. "Tell me now."

A slight pause, then, "That's 8:00 o'clock, sharp."

The line went dead.

Chapter 16

As Debbie opened the door to her suite, she heard her phone ringing. She threw her purse on the couch and grabbed the phone. "Hello?"

Silence.

The connection cut off.

Debbie slammed the phone down. "See if I run to answer you next time."

She looked at her watch. If she hurried, she still had time for a quick shower before tonight's performance.

Someone knocked on her door.

Shower or answer the door?

A second knock followed.

Persistent, aren't you? Debbie swung the door open.

Pam stepped in, pushing a roll-along suitcase. "I know I'm way early to touch up your hair and do your make-up, but I simply had to come. Guess what I found?" Pam flopped down on the couch.

"What?" Debbie tried to keep the irritation out of her voice.

Pam unzipped the suitcase, revealing a variety of hairbrushes, a curling iron, combs, sprays, and a make-up kit. She retrieved a book from the bottom of the suitcase and handed the book to Debbie. "It's our elementary school yearbook. Do you remember it?"

No, she didn't even know one existed. Grandma would have never bought one for her, so Debbie had paid little attention to such things.

"Go on, look at it. We're on page twenty-one, standing next to each other, like always."

Debbie glanced down at the thin book. Its mascot, a growling tiger, was embossed on its cover. She turned to page twenty-one and stared at the class picture. She barely recognized herself and the scrawny little girl next to her. She read the caption: . . . Deborah Gunther, Pamela Banis. . .

Pam. Rosey-cheeked Pam. Friendly.

"Looks like you finally remember me."

Debbie looked up. Had she been that obvious? "Of course I remember you."

"Good, 'cuz I did good by you today."

"Oh?"

"I did Melody's hair. I don't normally do hair that early, but she had a big important meeting at eight so I went to her house at 5:45 to do her hair. If you ask me, I'd say that's way too early. At least it's to me. How about you? Do you like to sleep late? I guess everybody does. So I'm doing her hair, right? And I get to talking to her and I casually mention how brave Dan was in saving Young Greg's life. I pointed out that her son's alive today only because of Dan's heroic deed. I tell her all of this just in case she hasn't put two and two together. Sometimes she's a little short in the common sense department, so I make it real clear. Then I tell her it's so noble of him not to want any money in return. All he wants is to find his little girl. Now, she didn't know anything about this, so I tell her all Dan wants is for her hubby to set up some contacts for him. Now I think that's only fair, I tell her. She agrees. By the time I finished with her, she was more than ready to go talk to her husband. So now Dan got what he wanted. I think he deserves it after all he did."

For the first time in a long time, Debbie felt a spark of hope. "That's wonderful. I know Dan will be happy to hear that."

The phone rang.

"Excuse me." Debbie retrieved the phone from its cradle. "Hello?"

Debbie could hear the person at the other end. It wasn't that the caller said anything or made any noise, but somehow Debbie knew someone was there.

"Hello?" Debbie recognized the exasperation on her voice.

Still, the silence remained.

Debbie slammed the phone down. "Don't people have anything better to do than play with the phone?"

"Why? Who was that?"

"Never did say. I don't have time to stand there and wait, so I hung up."

"Good for you. I hate those kind of calls. Bunch of teenagers, I bet you."

"Probably that's all it was." A chill covered her body. "That's the second time it's happened today."

"Yeah?"

"Yeah. The other was also a hang up. But like you said, it's probably a bunch of teeny boppers having fun."

But something told Debbie there was more to the calls than that. She tried to shrug it off but the thought dogged her, causing her stomach to do a flip.

Chapter 17

Dan glanced at his watch: 7:33. Damn, where had all the time gone? He still needed to polish that final story but knew that would have to wait.

He scooped his notes and disk into his briefcase and slammed it shut. Ever since he had received that call from Prickett, his powers of concentration had eluded him. He grabbed the suitcase and headed out.

As he turned to lock the office door, from the corner of his eye, Dan saw a tall, thin man quickly turn the corner. Dan had worked late many times before. Meeting deadlines often meant working odd hours. Yet, not once had he ever seen this man. Must be someone new. Poor sucker, just beginning and already staying late. In a way, it was comforting to know Dan wasn't the only fool who worked overtime—for no extra pay, he should add.

Dan rode the elevator down to the parking garage. Half of the spaces held compact cars with a few trucks and larger vehicles scattered here and there. Obviously, others also worked extended hours, maybe none on his floor, but definitely on the other—

Dan stopped.

He heard a scraping sound, like the shuffling of feet. He turned and confronted emptiness.

He quickened his pace and retrieved the keys to his car. The feeling that someone was watching him unnerved him. The urge to turn around and look enveloped him. Ten more large steps and he'd reach the safety of his car.

As he inserted the door key, Dan took a few seconds and scanned the area.

Deserted, except for him.

Still...

Dan opened the door, stepped in, turned the key, and somehow managed to get the car rolling without flooding it.

Through the rear view mirror, he saw the same tall, skinny man step out into the space he had just vacated, arms resting on his hips. He stared at Dan as he drove away.

* * *

"As far as I'm concerned, you're nothing more than an intruder in my home, so I'm not offering you anything to drink." Prickett sat behind his vast, oak desk cluttered with papers.

That's okay. I'm not even thirsty, Mr. Appreciative. "Is it all right to sit down?" Dan gestured toward the two wingback chairs resting on either side of him.

"Go ahead."

Dan sat but did not lean back. He folded his hands on his lap and felt like a midget in this high-ceilinged room.

"Before I tell you what you came here to hear, I need for you to clarify something for me. It's been bugging the hell out of me."

Bugging you? Why that's a good, little bug. Dan forced himself not to smile. He looked away from Prickett and concentrated on the leather-bound volumes that lined three walls. He wondered what kind of books appealed to Prickett. Obviously, the expensive kind.

"How did you know where to find my son? As many contacts as I have, not one seemed privileged to the knowledge you magically possessed."

Dan turned his gaze toward Prickett. "My informer told me."

"And that is?"

Some angel out there, trying to help me. "Heck if I know." Prickett frowned and Dan quickly continued, "That's one of my top priorities. I need to find who he is and talk to him. I feel he's got all this information I can tap."

"When you find him, I would like to talk to him."

"I'll pass that on to him."

Prickett's index fingers formed a steeple. He placed them under his chin. For a moment, he remained quiet, as though considering the alternatives. "Tell me why I shouldn't think you orchestrated my son's kidnaping, then gallantly saved him in order to gain what you want."

"I could have done that, but I didn't."

"Can you prove it?"

"No."

"No? That's it?"

"That's it."

Prickett studied Dan.

Dan tried not to move. He matched Prickett's glare with one of his own.

"You've got guts. I like that."

"I'm glad you're impressed." Dan continued to stare.

"You've also got a wise mouth, but assuming you did save my son, I'll let that pass. But if I find that you were in the least bit involved, I'll personally hunt you down. Is that clear?"

"Perfectly clear."

Prickett stood up and walked around his desk, closing the proximity between him and Dan. "I assume you keep up with the news."

"I try. It's part of my job. Are you referring to Elko Bloomer?"

Prickett folded his arms in front of him. "Unfortunate thing that happened to him."

"Worst part is that the chauffeur got caught in the middle, and he had to pay for Bloomer's mistakes."

"Don't let the chauffeur title fool you. He was the one who lured Young Greg into the limo."

Amazing how fast Prickett could gather information when he wanted to. Dan looked down at the plush, coppery carpet. He wished he were as lucky. His gaze traveled back up at Prickett who continued to scrutinize him. "So now they're both dead for their mistakes."

"Yes, and that's the unfortunate part—unfortunate for you, that is."

"Oh?"

"Seems that Bloomer was a greedy man. He wasn't happy being my second-in-command. He wanted more power, more money. It's always been my policy to leave drugs alone. I don't use them. I don't deal with them. They mess people up. You know what I mean?"

Dan couldn't think of what to say, so he nodded.

After a slight pause, Prickett continued, "The same follows for all of my employees. All, that is, except one. Bloomer, on his own, decided to expand his business to deal with drugs. He was underhanded and conniving. He kept that part of his life very well hidden from me." Prickett retrieved a cigarette from his shirt pocket. "Do you smoke?"

Dan shook his head.

"It's a filthy habit. I myself don't do it too much." He lit his cigarette and took a big puff. "Where was I?"

"You were telling me about Bloomer dealing with drugs."

"Yes, I was. Do you see where this is leading?"

"When I worked on that drug piece—and by the way, in all of my research, not once did Bloomer's name pop up."

"Of course it wouldn't. He was very careful to cover his tracks. He didn't want me finding out about his involvement. But he was still the top man."

How could Dan have missed this? That proved he wasn't as good of a reporter as he thought himself to be. Disgust filled him. "So he was the one who made the threatening calls?"

"No, not directly. But he's the one who ordered them."

"And those thugs, who came that night. Were they—"

Prickett nodded. "Bloomer sent them and ordered your wife's death and the baby's kidnapping."

Rage began to well up in Dan. He felt his blood pounding in his veins. Fighting for control, he clutched his fists into tight knots at his side. "Who were those men?" His words came out in short, angry rasps.

"There were two. One was a giant of a man. You met him."

Cosmo Grajeda.

Dan closed his eyes to keep the images from forming. An intimidating man, just by his size. A brute, by nature. What would Linda's last moments of life have been like?

He tried not to think, but the images of blood flashed before him. Linda's face swollen beyond recognition. Eight broken bones in her body, the medical examiner had later told him.

Yet, she had dragged herself down the hallway toward Diana's room. Always the concerned mother. The loving wife.

The blood.
The bruises.
The anguish.
The guilt.

Dan tightened his fists and fought for control. "And the other man?"

"An ordinary looking man by the name of Joe Watson. But looks can be deceiving. He had one hell of an evil streak on him."

Joe Watson? The name rang a bell. Where had he heard it? Of course. "The chauffeur."

"Exactly."

So Watson was dead. No big thing. At least Dan could still get the information he needed from Cosmo Grajeda. "How about setting up a meeting between Cosmo and me?"

"Impossible."

Dan glared at him. "You can't keep me from talking to him."

"Maybe I can't, but nature can." Prickett smiled at his own joke. "Soon as Bloomer heard that my son had been rescued, he flew back here to Las Vegas. He owns a private jet."

An unfortunate thing for Bloomer, but a lucky break for Prickett. "And?"

"First thing he did when he landed was kill Cosmo."

Damn! His two leads gone, just like that. "What about Diana?"

"Joe has a brother. Never met him, but he's a tall, skinny guy, if I remember right."

Dan sat up straighter.

Chapter 18

The audience awarded Debbie a standing ovation. That made the seventh one in a row. She smiled and threw the audience more kisses. If it were up to her, she'd kiss every single one of them. She felt that grateful.

She stepped back and the curtains dropped, separating her from her adoring fans. In less than two hours, she'd be back on stage again. Right now all she wanted to do was kick off her shoes off, flop down on bed, curl up with Rick Riordan's latest mystery, and get lost to the world.

Feeling gleeful, Debbie sprinted toward her suite.

She had barely locked the door behind her when the cell phone rang. She hoped it was Dan. He sometimes called between shows. "Hello?"

Silence, followed by heavy breathing.

Debbie held her breath. She was about to hang up when she heard a male voice say, "Tell Dan some things don't change. If he continues to poke around where he is now, you will die."

Debbie dropped the phone. She could feel her heart racing. Like an endless tape, the phrase repeated in her mind. "You will die...die...die..."

The more she thought about it, the more she felt her anger ready to erupt, like a volcano that had lain dormant for too long. She picked up the phone, ready to scream some obscenity at the caller, but all she heard was the dial tone.

* * *

At the midnight show, Debbie did not receive a standing ovation. As soon as the curtain dropped in front of her, she made a dash toward the exit door.

Someone grabbed her arm.

You will die...die...

With her breath in her throat, Debbie tried to focus on her attacker, but all she saw was the hand grasping her arm. From somewhere around her, she heard a familiar voice, "Relax, it's only me." The grasp tightened around her arm.

Debbie continued to stare at the hand that held her prisoner.

The grasp broke and Debbie felt like bolting. Unmasked fear forced her to remain glued to the spot.

"You're scaring me. Snap out of it. Are you okay?"

For the first time, Debbie saw the person standing beside her. "Bill. . ."

"I realize I'm not exactly the most handsome person in the world, but I didn't think I was that scary looking."

Debbie smiled at his feeble attempt to joke. "You startled me, that's all. I'm okay now."

"Mind telling me what just happened?"

"I. . .I got spooked." She widened her smile, trying to show him it wasn't important.

"Does this have something to do with what happened to you and Dan?"

Debbie knew he was referring to her previous life-threatening experience that centered on Colette's murder. Maybe that's why she spooked so easily. Maybe she hadn't quite gotten over the nightmares. She knew she had overreacted to a simple threatening call.

A simple threatening call? She almost had to smile at that one. She felt better. "I'm okay, really."

She had hoped that would ease Bill's concern, but the worry lines that creased the edge of his eyes did not disappear. "Listen, if you're having problems handling that experience, I can get you somebody to talk to. Don't be afraid to admit that there's a problem there. It's only natural."

"Thanks, but no. Like I said, I really am okay."

For a moment Bill remained quiet as his gaze penetrated Debbie's. "Don't misunderstand. This is strictly selfish. Tonight's last performance—although absolutely outstanding—didn't have that extra spark. As the director of your show, I'm responsible for its success. If anything is bothering you—anything at all—"

"I'll work it out." Debbie spotted Pam standing behind Bill. "I'm all right. Really." She wrinkled her nose, winked, and waved goodbye, just as Colette would have done.

She headed toward Pam.

"You look upset." Pam's tone was laced with concern. "Are you okay?"

"I need to talk to someone."

"I'm here if you need me."

Debbie hesitated. Would it really be wise to talk to Pam? But if she didn't talk to her, whom could she confide in? "Let's go get a drink." Debbie led her to one of the Crystal Palace Casino's bars. The Chandelier Disco lived up to its name. A giant chandelier lit up the area in such a way that it seemed to sprout tiny crystal drops on the bar, the tables, and the dance floor. Debbie chose a table back in the corner where they could talk quietly.

As they entered the bar, the band stopped playing. Debbie knew she had at least fifteen minutes of silence before the musicians returned from their break. Debbie used that time to tell Pam about that last call.

As she spoke, she noticed that off to her right, a tall, skinny man stared at her with all the warmth of a glacier.

Chapter 19

A familiar sound woke Dan up.

He opened one eye and cursed the alarm clock. It read 7:03. What had ever possessed him to set it for so early in the morning? He reached for the button that would turn it off.

It didn't work. The noise continued to infiltrate the room.

"What the..." He opened both eyes and tried to focus. That noise... The phone! He reached for it. "Hello." He felt surprised at how the word had come out sounding like a bark.

"Mr. Springer? Mr. Dan Springer?"

"Yes."

"I'm sorry to be waking you so early in the morning."

You better not be trying to sell me something, sweetie. Dan waited for her to continue.

"I'm a couple of miles away from your apartment, and I really would like to talk to you."

"What about?"

"Debbie."

"Sorry, I don't give interviews about her. You can reach her directly through the Crystal Palace Casino."

"I know how to reach Debbie. In fact, she and I are real good friends. Maybe she told you about me? My name is Pam. Pam Banis. There's something I need to tell you. Something I feel you should know."

All traces of sleep left Dan. "Do you know how to get to my place?"

"Yes, I can be there in about half-an-hour."

"I'll be waiting." Dan settled the phone in its cradle and jumped out of bed. He drew the drapes, allowing the sun's rays to filter in. The intense light forced him to squint. It promised to be another brilliant Las Vegas day, so typical of this city.

Dan splashed some water on his face, put some deodorant on, and rinsed his mouth with plain water. The first pair of pants that he grabbed would have to do. Good, just by luck it was his favorite pair, the faded blue jeans that fit just perfectly.

That sky-blue Polo shirt hanging over the chair needed to be worn. He hardly ever wore it because it didn't have a pocket. He hated shirts without pockets. He swore that after he took the shirt off today, he'd throw it away.

The shoes came next—the sloppy but comfortable pair.

The doorbell rang. "Jees! Half an hour, she said? It's only been ten minutes."

Barefooted, Dan looked out the window and was surprised to see Bronson. He opened the door.

"Good morning," Dan said.

Bronson nodded and stepped inside like he was exptected.

"Do I smell coffee brewing?"

"Yes, as a matter of fact I just turned the Mr. Coffee on."

"Ah, now that's quite an invention. I've got three of them at my place. Two of them so I always have a fresh pot available and a third in case one breaks down."

"You must really like coffee."

"I can't seem to function in the morning until I have at least two or three cups in me." He headed toward the kitchen.

Dan stuck his head out to see if he could spot a young woman who might turn out to be Pam. He saw two runners and an elderly man walking his sheltie. He closed the door and joined Bronson in the kitchen who was searching for a cup.

Dan opened the dishwasher and retrieved two clean cups. "So what brings you over here?"

Dan poured Bronson a cup. His face brightened.

"I have a couple of hazy areas in my notes. I wanted to clear them up, if you don't mind."

As a matter of fact, he minded. He didn't want to answer any more questions. "Go ahead."

Bronson retrieved his notebook and fired away while Dan finished pouring himself a cup of coffee. They took their cups to the den and after answering Bronson's questions, Dan filled him in on his latest findings. He finished by telling Bronson about the tall, skinny man. "He just stood there in the parking lot, looking at me. If I'd known who he was, I would have turned back."

"So you're thinkin' maybe this man is your informer."

"More than likely."

"The informer's voice, you said, was deep. Describe deep."

Dan searched his mind. He could do this. He was a man of words, wasn't he? "Hoarse. You know, lowered on purpose."

"Would you say throaty?"

After considering it, Dan nodded. "Yeah, throaty would be a good word."

The doorbell rang and Dan welcomed the interruption.

A brunette who stood about five-six stared at Dan through brown, liquid eyes. "Mr. Springer? Mr. Dan Springer?"

He nodded.

"I called you. I'm Pam. Pam Banis."

Dan opened the door wider and Pam stepped in. She sucked in her breath when she saw Bronson. "I'm sorry. I didn't know you had company."

"Not his fault, ma'am. I just popped in unexpectedly. I'm Detective Harry Bronson." He looked down at his coffee cup. "I'm empty. If you excuse me, I think I'll get me a refill. Dan, would you like for me to refill yours?"

Dan looked at his nearly full cup and shook his head.

"No, I'm fine.".

"How about you, ma'am? Would you care for some?"

"No, thank you. I can only stay a few minutes."

Bronson walked out and Pam turned to Dan. "Has Debbie told you anything about me? We went to school together back when we were little. Back then, I was this shy little girl, and so was Debbie. But even then she had something magical about her. I could tell. That's what drew me to her. I think it was. . .charisma. Yes, that's it. Now look at her. She's a big, famous movie star."

Dan pointed to the couch and Pam nodded. She sat down and continued her narrative. "She's not really a movie star. I know that, but she'll get there. That beautiful voice of hers. It's a shame she has to impersonate Colette. I mean, she does a fabulous Colette. Everybody knows that, but that's not what she was born to do. She—"

"Ma'am, is that what you wanted to tell Dan?" Bronson, holding his cup of coffee, leaned against the wall. His eyes pierced Pam's.

"No, of course not. It's just that I'm...nervous. I feel—"

Bronson set his coffee down on the stereo unit and walked toward Pam. "No need, ma'am, to be nervous. You're among friends."

"But. . . but you're the police." Pam bit her lip.

"Don't let that frighten you, ma'am. I'm a detective in Dallas, but here I'm just a tourist. Would it help if I step back into the kitchen?"

"No. If you're a friend of Dan's and a detective too, I think Dan—as well as me—can benefit from your expertise. Frankly, I'm afraid for Debbie."

"And why would that be?" Bronson asked before she could utter another word.

"She's gotten some calls."

An icy chill came over Dan. "What kind of calls?"

"Hang-ups, mostly. We thought it was kids at first—well, teens, actually—you know, playing on the phone. Debbie tells me don't they have better things to—"

"That last call wasn't a hang up." Bronson took a sip of coffee.

Pam's eyebrows arched. "No, it wasn't, but how did you know that?"

"My gut told me. I make it a point to always listen to my gut. Tell us everything you can remember about this last call."

"I wasn't there for that one. I got this from Debbie. Last night, she was very shook up. Her midnight performance was even a bit off and her string of standing ovation was broken. Bill—that's her director—he noticed it, too. He grabbed her after the show and Debbie freaked out. I guess she was thinking about the call. Bill told her—"

"Ma'am, about the call."

"Oh sure. Like I said, I wasn't there, but Debbie told me he said that if Dan didn't stop, she was going to die."

"Dammit!" Dan bolted up from the sofa. "Why didn't she tell me?"

"She's afraid of how you're going to react. She thinks that maybe you will push her away. She wants to be by your side, just like you were by her side when she was being stalked by Colette's killer."

"That's different. My life wasn't in danger."

"That's not what she says. Worst thing you can do now is push her away from you. She needs you. Don't let her down." Pam stood up. "I knew you'd want to know, and I also knew Debbie probably wouldn't tell you for fear you'll dump her. So please don't tell her I told you. She'll be furious with me, but I'm so afraid for her, I had to let you know."

"You did the right thing. I appreciate you telling me."

Pam nodded. "I just don't want to see her getting hurt."

"I won't let her get hurt. I promise."

"Good. I'll let you two get back to whatever you were doing. . . . Dan, it was nice meeting you. Debbie's told me a lot about you. Detective—"

"I think you're a true friend." Bronson scratched his chin. "Heck, I know you are. You've said you've known her since the third grade. That's a long time to know somebody. You kept in touch all these years, have you?"

"Not exactly. My family moved, and I went to a different high school. We promised each other we'd keep in touch, but you know how that goes. Shortly after high school, Debbie became a celebrity, and I've read everything that's ever been written about her. I even read your article, Dan. Very well done."

"Thanks."

She turned to leave.

"One more thing." Bronson retrieved his notebook from his pocket and scribbled something down.

She stopped.

"Debbie told you that last call definitely came from a man, not a woman."

"That's correct."

"And the other calls? She didn't say anything about them, other than that they were hang-ups. Was it the same guy who made the calls?"

"I suppose so, but I can't be sure."

"Both of you assumed the earlier calls came from teenagers. Why was that? Were there giggles on the other end of the line?"

"I don't think so. Debbie didn't say anything like that. It was just something we just kind of assumed, you know what I mean?"

"Aha." Bronson took off his glasses, blew some air onto the right lens and wiped it with his handkerchief. "I was thinkin'." He cleaned the other lens.

Awfully slow process, this thinking, Dan wanted to say. He bit his tongue.

Bronson put his glasses back on and stuffed the handkerchief in his pocket. "The way I see it, you don't want Debbie to know we—or more appropriately, Dan—know that you told us about the calls. But I'd like to put some listening devices in her living room, bedroom, and possibly kitchen. This way if she gets in trouble, we can immediately respond. Can you help us?"

Alarm registered in Pam's eyes. "How?"

"Sometime when Debbie is busy like maybe tonight when she's performin', you can let us in her suite. Dan and I can do the work."

"I don't see how." Pam's gaze bounced around the room as though searching for a way. She shrugged. "I don't have access to her suite. I'm her hairdresser and make-up artist, so she needs to be there when I'm there. No reason for me to have a key."

"But you can borrow the key from someone?"

"Like who?"

Bronson frowned. "I was hopin' you'd be able to tell me that."

"I don't even know how to go about arranging that, but I suppose I can ask around if you want me to."

Bronson shook his head. "No, I don't want anyone knowin' the place is bugged. Just us three." He formed a fist and blew into it. "It was just a thought anyway." He turned to Dan. "I'll walk Ms. Pam out while you go make a fresh pot of coffee. I just drank the last cup."

Dan cringed at Bronson's order. *Do I look like a frickin' maid?* He picked up the empty cup and stormed off to the kitchen. He rinsed the pot, dumped out the old grinds, and scooped some coffee out of the can. When he looked up, Bronson was leaning on the kitchen counter.

"It will just be a minute."

"Sorry to be such a pain-in-the-ass."

Dan shrugged. "You don't need to bother Pam about a key to Debbie's suite. I have a key."

"I figured you did." Bronson poured three packets of sugar in his empty cup. "My Carol—she hates me using so much sugar in my coffee. Used to be I put four packets. Now, I'm down to three. Maybe soon I'll go down to two. Or maybe two-and-a-half. What you think?"

"I think bugging Debbie's place is an excellent idea. Can you really do it?"

"Wouldn't have offered if I couldn't." Bronson bent down and looked anxiously at the brewing coffee.

"Then let's."

"I'll get the stuff. It'll be done by tomorrow. I'll need Debbie's key or you can come with me."

"I have a question."

"I have an answer."

"Don't you want to hear the question first?"

"Fine by me."

"If you knew I had a key to Debbie's suite, why did you ask Pam if she had one?"

"How else would I know if she had access to Debbie's suite anytime she wanted to?"

"Oh. . . . I see."

"Glad you do." Bronson smiled as the coffee maker completed its job. He poured himself a cup and headed for the door. "I best be goin'. My Carol is probably at that keno machine. Why would anybody go invent a game like that anyway?"

"When Nevada banned the use of the lottery, a lot of people got quite upset. So several versions of keno sprang up to make up for it."

Bronson's eyebrows arched. "Oh really? And here I thought it was to hook my Carol and make me go broke."

"Well, I'll be happy to pay you for time. I just don't want Debbie to get hurt."

"Nah, protectin' people is what I do and I'd do it for nothing if I didn't like eatin' so much. Fortunately the fine citizens of Dallas provide me with an ample salary."

As exasperating as Bronson sometimes could be, Dan felt a genuine liking for this man. "Thanks."

"Don't mention it." Bronson took one more swig of coffee. He emptied his cup and shoved it toward Dan. "Okay, I'm out of here."

Bronson let himself out just as he had let himself in. At the door, he paused. "Did you notice how Ms. Pam admitted meeting Debbie in the third grade?" He frowned and shook his head. "I could have sworn you told me it was the second grade." Again, Bronson tapped his forehead, but this time it was in the form of a salute. "Have a good day. See you later."

Chapter 20

Dan stood in the doorway staring at Bronson's vanishing figure. Pam had said third grade in today's conversation. Prior to that, she had said second grade. Did that make a difference? What was Bronson driving at anyway? Dan gently closed the door, headed to the kitchen, and placed a frozen ham and egg sandwich in the microwave.

As Dan ate his breakfast, he thought about Bronson's unusual comments. He thought about Pam as he cleaned the dishes and later, shaved and showered. She had seemed so sincere about not wanting to see Debbie hurt. Had she been maybe a little too sincere? Was it all an act? Is that what Bronson tried to tell him?

Dan cursed Bronson for speaking in circles. Why couldn't the man come straight out and say what he meant? Dan grabbed the car keys and sped off toward the Crystal Palace Casino.

* * *

As Dan drove down the famous Strip, more than thirty wedding chapels shouted at him. They ranged from elaborate to downright tacky. He briefly wondered which one would appeal to Debbie.

None, he decided. If and when they got married, it would be in a traditional church.

He pulled into the Crystal Palace Casino's parking lot and found a spot adjacent to one of the many flowerbeds that made the casino famous. The morning greeted him with one set of blooms. He knew that an entirely different array would await him in the afternoon.

He hurried past the fountain with bronze life-size statues of royalty reclining in the pools. The statues watched their playful children cast water at one another. Depending on which angle the light hit the water; it made it seem as though the princes and princesses threw crystals at each other instead of water drops.

Dan stepped into the casino's stately entrance consisting of polished blue and white marble. The gilded woodwork and glittering chandeliers did not attract his attention. Neither did the constant clink of coins dropping in the slot machines' bins. Instead, he headed for the elevators and to the top floor, which housed Debbie's suite.

Even though Dan had a key to the suite, he knocked and waited. When no one answered, Dan let himself in. Hot, queasy panic churned in his stomach. No logical reason existed why Debbie should be waiting for him in her suite, but still...

Where was she?

Was she all right?

"Hi, handsome."

Dan turned. "Debbie! Thank God you're all right."

"Did he call you, too?"

"What?"

Debbie sank into the couch. "I debated whether I should say anything. Now I have no choice." She told him about the phone calls she'd been receiving.

As Dan listened quietly, his mind boiled with turmoil. Should he tell her he already knew about the calls? As a journalist, he believed in the Bill of Rights with the same fervor as he believed in the Ten Commandments. He would support both. No doubt in his mind. His commitment to the First Amendment dictated the he must protect his source. That meant deceiving Debbie. He simply couldn't let her know he already knew about the calls.

The other part of him, the one that tugged at his heart, was what made him a man. As such he felt fiercely loyal to

Debbie, wanting with all his heart to share even the smallest of secrets with her.

She finished her narrative and still the two sides of Dan struggled for control. He felt Debbie tense, and he knew he had to make a decision. The journalist won.

He wrapped his arms around her. "I'm sorry I brought this on you." He kissed her forehead, wishing he could make the man go away. "Other than the calls, has anything else happened?"

Debbie shook her head.

"Nobody's following you?"

Again, she shook her head.

"No strangers lurking around?"

God, he was beginning to sound like Bronson. He had already asked that question. Why was he repeating himself?

When Debbie failed to answer, he began to understand why Bronson insisted on repeating everything. This time it was his turn. "Tell me about the stranger."

Debbie smiled a bit self-consciously. "It's probably nothing."

"I still want to know."

"Last night I was talking to Pam at the bar down in the casino. A man came in and sat across the bar from us. He kept looking at me. In my kind of job, that's not unusual. What was different was the way he kept staring. I felt as if he wanted to hurt me. He gave me the creeps." Debbie shook herself and rubbed her upper arms with her hands as though trying to dispel the feeling.

"What did this man look like?"

"Tall and skinny, with beady eyes. I know that doesn't sound very intimidating. It's just that...I don't know."

An image flashed in Dan's mind. The man in his rear view mirror, tall and skinny. "I think I know who he is." Dan told Debbie what Prickett had said. "If he is Joe Watson's brother—and if Prickett is telling the truth about Watson being one of the two men who...who..."

Debbie threw her arms around Dan.

He looked away, not wanting to see the compassion that Debbie's features displayed. "I'm...I'm sorry. It still hurts to talk about it." He rubbed his eyes.

"I know. I'm sorry too." She kissed his forehead.

He kissed her lips. Even now with the pain stabbing at his heart, Dan realized how much he wanted—and needed—Debbie.

Later. Definitely later. He stood up. "I know what I've got to do."

"And that is?"

"I'm going to let him find me."

Chapter 21

Dan picked up his cell phone and punched in Bronson's number. "Debbie will be rehearsing for the next two to three hours. I thought maybe we could use that time to wire the place. Will that give us enough time?"

"More than enough. Be there in ten minutes."

Nine minutes later, Dan opened the door and Bronson stood there sipping a cup of coffee he'd managed to get from a vending machine on way there. Dan let him in and they immediately got to work. From the brown paper bag he carried, he retrieved rubber-handled pliers, a small screwdriver, and two electrical outlet plates. He sat on the floor and started removing the cover plate that was already there. "This here thing may look like an ordinary wall plug, but it's got listening devices build into it. It runs off wires and don't need batteries. They're the best." Using long-nosed pliers, he clamped off the wires. "I'll be able to listen from my car or motel room. I hear somethin', I'll be here as fast as a hummingbird flies."

He finished the living room and repeated the procedure in the bedroom. "She has the radio or TV on often?"

"Not really."

"Good, she turns them on, I won't be able to hear."

"Think maybe we should tell her what we've done?"

"I reckon you should."

He picked up his tools and headed out the door.

* * *

The hot summer sun that makes Las Vegas a year-round attraction refused to shine. Instead, a heavy overcast settled over the City of Lights, casting a gloomy spell. This is a typical day for a funeral, Dan thought as he slowed down and joined the precession heading to Evergreen Restlawn.

The line of cars, mostly limousines, BMW's, Porches and a handful of black Mercedes Benzes formed a line that spilled past the cemetery's gate and out onto Eastern Avenue. Once Dan maneuvered a left turn into the cemetery, he realized the line was a lot longer than he had originally anticipated.

A wide driveway curved past a waterfall where iron ducks frolicked in the water. A quaint, colossal chapel, several hundred yards away from the cascades provided not only comfort and hope, but also added a touch of serenity. Off the driveway, several roads led down to well-groomed lawns filled with colorful flowers. This was where most of Las Vegas's richest citizens were buried.

But not Bloomer. For people like him, who were considered more than just wealthy, another area was reserved. Behind the chapel, private mausoleums that resembled smaller versions of mansions majestically encircled a large pond.

As Dan waited for his turn to park, he watched the funeral's attendees as they gathered behind the blue velvet, padded chairs located under a huge blue canopy. All of the chairs were already occupied except for the one in the middle of the front row.

When his turn came, Dan parked his green Honda CRV behind a Cadillac from which a young man wearing a dark suit escorted an elderly lady dressed in an elegant, yet casual black ankle-length dress. Dan briefly wondered who they were. He watched them as they joined the rest of the crowd.

Casting his gaze toward the cemetery plot, Dan wished he knew what connection all these people had to Elko Bloomer. If he could talk to each one of them, would he learn anything new about his daughter?

"So I see you read old detective novels, huh?"

Dan turned and faced Bronson. He wore a dark gray shirt that had seen better days and a pair of dress black slacks that didn't seem to fit too well. "What do you mean?"

"The hero of the story always attends the funeral and studies all the mourners, and suddenly he knows who the culprit is."

Dan smiled. "Is that why you're here?"

"I reckon you could say that. It may be a cliché, but it works. Maybe that's why it is a cliché."

By now they had reached the rest of the crowd. They stood off to the side, apart from the others. Dan followed Bronson's gaze as it lingered on someone, then darted to the next person, then on to the next. "Just exactly who is it that you're looking for?"

"At this point, I'm not sure. I'm just lookin' to be lookin'. What about you? What brought you here?"

"Guilt." As illogical as it seemed, Dan couldn't help but think that Elko Boomer wouldn't be dead if he hadn't rescued Young Greg.

"Ah, yes. Always a most powerful motive. Thing is though, if you hadn't intervened, chances are that it would have been Young Greg who would have been buried today. Think about that when you start feelin' guilty."

Dan watched Bronson walk away from him. Damn, if he wasn't right. Part of the guilt seemed to evaporate like fog lifting from the road. Dan continued to watch Bronson as he moved from place to place, briefly stopping to study, analyze. When Dan lost sight of Bronson, he turned his attention to the people around him.

Much to his disappointment, he didn't spot the tall, skinny man he desperately wanted to find. He considered turning around and leaving, but many people were still arriving, and there was still a chance that the thin man would show up. Dan could see no harm in waiting.

All heads turned as the black limousine drove up. The chauffeur opened the back door, and Barbara slipped out. She wore a long, black dress that clung to her curves. The collar had been turned up, adding just the right touch of elegance. The lack of jewelry played down its stunning effect. Large designer sunglasses covered her eyes.

She paused briefly by the car's open door, whispered something to the chauffeur, and with her head held high, headed for the seat that awaited her by the gravesite. A dozen selected family members and friends were already sitting down, waiting for her arrival. Without acknowledging them, she took her place in the front row. The people who had cleared a path for Barbara closed in, blocking Dan's view of her.

"After the services, there's a handful of selected people who will gather at Ms. Bloomer's residence."

Dan turned to face a rather young looking man whom he immediately recognized as the new chauffeur. "I only know Ms. Bloomer as a brief, business acquaintance. Please pass my condolences to her."

"You can do that yourself when you see her at the Bloomer Palace after the funeral," the chauffeur said.

"No, not me. I'm afraid I'm not one of the few selected to attend the private, grieving affair."

"That's where you're wrong, Mr. Springer. Ms. Bloomer specifically requested your presence."

Something clicked in Dan's mind, a warning bell, perhaps. He took a step away from the chauffeur and scanned the area for Bronson. He was nowhere in sight. "I'm afraid I won't be going."

"Wrong, again." The chauffeur shoved a gun into the small of Dan's back.

"On second thought, I think I'll go."

Chapter 22

Rather curious, Bronson thought.

Dan had left with Ms. Bloomer's chauffeur at the beginning of the service. Both the limousine and Dan's car remained where they had been originally parked.

Bronson assumed Dan had wanted to stay for the entire service. After all, his main purpose was to seek the tall, skinny man. For that, he needed to be present. Yet he had gotten inside a red Taurus driven by a man Bronson had not recognized. Both Dan and the chauffeur had slipped into the back seat and the driver sped off.

Most curious indeed.

* * *

For the second time within the week, Dan found himself entering the Bloomer Palace's driveway. This time, however, the guard waved them right in, and instead of stopping at the front of the mansion, the driver swung around the back.

"You will wait for Ms. Bloomer in there." The chauffeur pointed to the structure behind Bloomer's Palace.

"You wait for Ms. Bloomer there, and I'll wait in the main house where it'll be a lot more comfortable." Dan turned, heading toward the main residence.

The chauffeur yanked Dan's arm and shoved him toward the guesthouse. "Need I remind you that I'm the one with the gun?"

"Good point. I think I'll make myself comfortable in the guesthouse. Do you think she'll mind if we turn on the TV?"

The chauffeur ignored him and shoved him toward the den. "Sit."

Dan chose a thick, leather chair facing the fireplace. At the center of the mantle, a decorative desk clock ticked the minutes away. Dan busied himself studying the original paintings on the wall. As he focused on the first oil painting, he noticed that the chauffeur stood by the entry and that he no longer carried the gun. But that didn't fool Dan. He knew that it remained within easy reach.

Another guard joined them. He walked clear across the room and sat in the far corner of the room, staring at Dan.

If luck accompanied him, Dan might be able to rush one guard, but he could never do both. So he focused on the paintings and prayed he could find a way out.

Almost an hour later, the door opened and Barbara stepped in still dressed in black.

"Excuse me for not rising, but I'm afraid your guards might misinterpret my intent."

"I like that in a man." Barbara headed toward him and stood directly in front of him. "Even under trying circumstances, you keep your sense of humor. Let's see how long that's going to last."

"Why? What do you have in mind?"

"Two things, actually. One, I have a task for you." As she spoke, she kept her gaze focused on him.

"What kind of a task?"

"The last time you and your friend—Marcos, wasn't it?"

Dan remained noncommittal.

Barbara flashed him a victory smile. The bitch. He'd have to be careful not to reveal anything else.

Barbara raised her head slightly in defiance to his silence. "The last time both of you were here, you made a fool of me. You used me to get to Young Greg, and I don't appreciate being made a fool."

"Would it help if I apologized?"

"Hardly, under the circumstances. My father is dead, you know, and you are partly responsible for that."

Dan closed his eyes and looked away. Right now, he didn't think much of himself.

Barbara sat down on the couch adjacent to him. "I'm hurting. I didn't realize it would hurt this much. My father might not have been a law-abiding man and for that, I can never forgive him. But he was my father, gentle and kind to me. Always."

She paused in an obvious effort to keep her composure. "I want to avenge my father's death." Her eyes burned with a fierceness that startled Dan.

Dan started to protest, but Barbara waved him off. "Both you and I know who's responsible for my father's death. But Prickett will never see one day in prison for what he's done." She stood up and once again Barbara's gaze pierced Dan's. "They say the pen is mightier than the sword. You have the pen. I want you to expose Prickett for what he is."

Frustration mixed with regret formed a tight knot in Dan's stomach. "I need Prickett's help—"

"—to find your daughter."

Unable to think of anything to say, Dan nodded.

"You're surprised. I can see it in your face." She sat back down. "As you can see, I've done my homework. You expose Prickett in such a way that he will have to be punished for my father's death. Once that is done, then your slate will be clean with me. I will never forgive you, but at least I know you did the right thing."

"I need time to think."

"You don't understand. This is not a request. This is an order. I am not an evil person. Unlike my father, I live by the law and hated that part of him that was bad. However, for this, I'm making an exception. You will expose Prickett, and you will do it within a reasonable amount of time."

Barbara walked over to the bar and fixed herself a drink. "Debbie is such a beautiful woman. If anything ever happened to her face, do you think she would be able to continue with her career? And what about Marcus and his wife, Stephanie? She's still very young. And the kids. So cute and defenseless too, you know?" She flashed him a smile as insincere as it was ugly.

Dan felt anger envelope him. "You wouldn't dare."

"Oh, wouldn't I?" She swirled her drink, stared at it, took a sip, and set it down. "It's your call. You expose him, and no one other than Prickett will get hurt. You have my word on that." She grabbed her drink and headed toward Dan. "I'll even sweeten the pot for you." She took another sip. "I will personally hand you your informer."

"You know who he is?"

A long silence stretched between them. She remained standing, looking down at Dan. Her posture, her manner revealed nothing. The original ice lady. Dan bit his lip and felt his stomach churn.

Slowly, she nodded.

Dan thought of the tall, skinny man. "Who is he?"

"In time and only after you have dealt with Prickett."

Dan sank deeper into the chair. At least he wasn't going to be killed. Or at least not yet. "Lucky for you, I believe in justice, and if Prickett is responsible for your father's death, then I agree that he should be exposed." How he was going to accomplish this and manage to survive he wasn't quite sure, but he'd take it one step at a time. "Am I free to leave?"

"Not just yet. If you remember, I told you there were two things. We already discussed the first. The second, I'm afraid, you won't like at all."

As if he liked the first.

"You noticed I did not offer you a drink."

As a matter of fact, he had noticed.

"That's because alcohol deadens the senses. When my bodyguards teach you a lesson about setting up my father for his death, I want you to feel everything."

What Others Know

Shit. She was right. He wasn't going to like that at all.

Barbara moved toward the door and stopped. She looked at her chauffeur but spoke loud enough so Dan could hear her. "Remember, I want him punished for what he did, but stop short of hospitalization. And don't damage his hands. He must be able to write those stories."

She turned to face Dan. "This will not make my pain go away, but it will certainly help." She opened the door, let herself out, and two husky-looking men stepped in.

All four men headed toward Dan.

Oooh shit!

Dan bolted out of the chair and braced himself.

Chapter 23

Less than a minute later the door reopened.

The men moved apart and Dan saw Barbara standing in the doorway. Had she come to watch the slaughter?

She took a step forward and to the right. Dan could now see a man standing behind her. Barbara moved again and Dan had a clear view of him. Relief flooded through his veins. Bronson was just the person he wanted to see.

Bronson stepped forward and Dan caught a view of Bronson's backup, his niece. Sylvia looked splendid in her full uniform.

Bronson looked his way and arched his eyebrows. "Why, Mr. Springer, what are you doing here?"

Dan stepped around the men. "I just finished my interview, and now I'm ready to head out. Bad thing is, I don't have my car. Can I impose on you to give me a ride?"

"I suppose so." Bronson fished the keys out of his pocket and looked at Barbara, "Ma'am, I'll be in touch and my condolences to you."

With that Bronson, Sylvia, and Dan walked out. Dan felt like bolting for the door, but instead he followed Bronson and Sylvia's lead.

They strolled out of the mansion as if they were heading for a leisurely evening walk.

Once inside the car, Dan felt like Atlas must have felt when he no longer had to carry the world. "How did you pull that off?"

"It's amazing what a badge can do."

"It's a Dallas badge."

"But Sylvia's isn't. I simply flashed them mine and they assumed it was as good as Sylvia's. Not my fault."

Dan smiled. He knew Bronson and Sylvia had taken a big risk. "I appreciate what you both did."

Sylvia raised her hand and waved it as though dismissing the subject. "Don't mention it. As you know, I'm still patrolling the streets, but this is the kind of stuff I love to do. I got a great adrenaline rush from this."

"Glad to hear that." Bronson handed Dan the car keys. "You're about to get another rush. Dan is driving."

* * *

Even before Dan reached his desk at work, Marcus handed him a note. "Prickett called. He wants to talk to you ASAP."

Dan looked at the paper and his nerves tingled. "Okay, thanks."

He settled into his comfortable work chair. Years ago, he had purchased the plush swivel chair with his own money. He knew he'd spend a lot of hours there, either doing interviews over the phone, surfing the net for research and ideas, or pounding on the keyboard in order to produce the articles prior to the deadlines.

Today, the chair felt stiff and formal.

Prickett picked up on the second ring. "Took you long enough to return my call."

Hello to you, too. This had turned out to be one hell of a day. "Do you have any more information for me?"

"I have someone right here in my office, you'll want to hear what he has to say. He's growing rather impatient, so if I were you, I'd get over here as soon as possible."

"I'm on my way." Dan bolted out of the chair even before he cradled the phone. "I'm on my way to Prickett's office," he told Marcus who had quit working and concentrated on Dan.

"Will you be okay? Want me to go with you?"

"I'll be fine. No use both of us falling behind on our articles."

"Party pooper."
"That's me."

* * *

Water gushed over the boulders and spilled into a small pool. Flowers of various colors and shapes blossomed around the water. So typical of Las Vegas, Dan thought. A desert filled with flowers and man-made waterfalls everywhere. Perhaps people were trying to bring back the era when the Las Vegas valley thrived with lush green vegetation.

Dan saw the wrought iron sign that read Prickett Park. He turned off Desert Inn Road into the narrow entryway of Prickett Park. From there, the area unfolded into a large cul-de-sac housing three five-story, all-glass buildings. The same kind of flowers that grew out front adorned pathways to the buildings and to the picnic benches. Large shade trees provided comfort from the often-glaring hot Las Vegas sun.

Dan parked his car in one of the two oversized parking lots and headed to the third floor of the main building, where he knew Prickett waited for him. Dan barely paid attention to the original paintings and bronze statues that added a touch of elegance to the office.

A young woman with rich, black eyes greeted Dan. "You must be Mr. Springer." She stood up, revealing a tight fitting red dress. She rivaled the Las Vegas showgirls, and Dan briefly wondered if Prickett had hired her strictly for her looks or for her secretarial skills. "Mr. Prickett wants me to show you in as soon as you arrived. Please follow me."

She led him down the corridor and to the right. Although he tried not to, Dan found his gaze focused on her swinging hips. He'd follow her anywhere.

She opened the door and Dan stepped in, past the two bodyguards standing like soldiers on duty by the door.

Immediately Prickett rose from behind his large, mahogany desk. "We'll be more comfortable over here." He pointed to his left, an area that looked more like a living room than an office.

    Sitting in the middle of the richly upholstered couch, a man with bent shoulders sat looking down at the magazine he held in his hands. He turned the page, but Dan could tell he wasn't paying attention. The tall, skinny man looked up at Dan.

Chapter 24

"I believe this is the man you've been wanting to talk to." Prickett led Dan toward the reception part of his office. "Dan Springer, I'd like you to meet Derek Watson."

Dan looked past the two bodyguards who by now stationed themselves by Prickett's desk and at the man he immediately recognized. He shook Derek's sweaty hand and sat across from him. "You've been following me."

Derek averted his gaze. "Uh...well...yeah, I guess so."

"Why?"

"I, uh, wanted to talk to you, but I didn't know if that was really the smart thing to do. So I followed you. I wanted to know what kind of person you were, uh, are."

"You also followed Debbie."

"Well, yeah. She's your lady. That way I'd get a real clear picture of you."

"Why would you care what kind of person I am?"

"I, uh, have something that used to, uh, belong to you."

"And that is?"

"Your...daughter."

The world fell out from under Dan. A rush of emotions bombarded him all at once—happiness, trepidation, joy, anguish, hope, and confusion. "Where is she? I want to see her."

Derek took out his wallet and retrieved a picture. With shaking hands, he handed the photograph to Dan.

A rush of excitement over came Dan as he stared at the face of the toddler in the photo. The light brown, almond-shaped eyes were familiar. These were his eyes. But the rest of her face, the delicate features, the slightly up-turned chin, the wide forehead—those were Linda's.

Deep sorrow settled in quickly. So many lost years. He stroked her image. "Diana."

"Lydia."

Dan was enraged by this intrusion into his private moment between his daughter and him. He looked up. "What?"

"Her name is Lydia."

No, she didn't look like a Lydia. Diana was small and dainty, like Linda. Dan set the picture down on the coffee table. He lifted his eyes to Derek. "I want to see her."

"That's, uh, impossible. My wife—she, uh—"

"I don't give a damn about your wife. I want to see my daughter." He grasped the armrests so tightly that he felt the blood drain away from his hands.

Prickett handed Dan a drink. "It'd be best if you listen to his story. This isn't easy for him either."

Dan grabbed the drink. Scotch and water. He didn't like Scotch and water. He took a swig anyway, set the glass down, and leaned back. "Go on."

Derek looked up at Prickett who gave him an encouraging nod. Derek rubbed his chin in an obvious effort to control himself. "First of all, I, uh, want to apologize for breaking into your apartment."

Dan stiffened.

"I . . . I didn't do nothing. I didn't touch nothing. I didn't take nothing. I just over-turned that lamp. I knew that if I did that, you'd get the message."

"You were there that night. You son-of-a-bitch!" Dan sprang out of his chair, ready to attack Derek.

Derek gasped and shrunk back.

The two bodyguards sprang toward Dan and held him back.

A frown formed on Prickett's forehead. "There's no need for that, Mr. Springer. We're civilized people here. Sit down and listen to Derek's story."

Dan straightened his shirt and sat down.

"To answer your question, no, I wasn't there the night your wife was murdered. I just know about it." Derek rubbed his face with a trembling hand. "I broke in so that if I had to tell you this story, you'd know I was speaking the truth. Maybe I was hoping to scare you off too." He looked away and nervous fingers swept his mouth. "But before we get to your wife's murder, let's go back to the beginning."

Derek leaned back and for a moment, he remained quiet. His eyes glistened as if he were crying. "My wife—her name is Lydia, too. She, uh, couldn't have any kids. And that was her dream—our dream—you know. To have children. Lots and lots of them." His gaze shifted to the picture and remained there for what Dan considered an eternity. "One day, Joe—that's my brother—came to visit. Somehow we got talking about kids and Lydia burst our crying. My poor brother, he took pity on Lydia, and promised her he'd deliver a baby.

"'In nine months from now, you'll have your baby,' he said. 'Use these months to make any preparations you want.'

"Well, now, my Lydia took him seriously. She started telling all her friends that she was pregnant. Soon after that, she started wearing a pillow. She even went as far as getting one of those things that actresses use to make them look pregnant. She really looked like she was going to have a baby. Nobody could tell the difference." He cast his eyes downward, his head tilted wearily against his hand.

"Then, when she was supposedly seven months along, we moved. We told everyone we were going to visit her parents. But instead we rented an isolated cabin close to

Ruidoso, New Mexico. Nobody knew us there. We stayed pretty much to ourselves. Three months went by and still no baby. Lydia was beside herself. She spent the entire time crying and cursing." A hollow, anguished expression filled his face, and he looked away, but not before Dan saw the tears form at the rim of his eyes. Using the palms of his hands, he wiped his eyes with short angry strokes.

"Then the call came. Some hotshot reporter had written a set of articles about the drug trade here in Las Vegas. Elko Bloomer—that's my brother's boss—he was plenty mad. He tried warning him to stop, but he wouldn't. So he ordered my brother and another guy to go into the reporter's house and take the baby. Elko meant to give the baby back after the reporter—that's you, I reckon—killed the series. But my brother, he had other plans. He convinced Elko that keeping the baby for insurance was the best way to go. 'He'll never release those articles, for fear of what'll happen to the baby,' my brother told him." Derek slumped back into the couch as though trying to retreat into the shadows.

Dan sat perfectly still. He must keep control of his emotions. Hear the man out. Derek took the baby away from him, but it was Dan's foolish pride that made it possible for him to keep her. If he hadn't insisted on writing those articles…

"We gave her a good home. We loved her as no other parents could love a child. She blossomed under our gentle care into this beautiful child." Again he looked at the picture and this time the tears spilled out of his eyes. "Then, when she was four…" The sound of his anguished sigh filled the room.

Dan felt like a child, waiting for the crack of a whip. "Diana!" The whispered word shouted Dan's urgency.

"She's…dead."

Chapter 25

Now, more than ever, Dan needed Debbie. He had sat like a zombie listening to Derek's strained voice. The tears that begged to be released had not come. Dan locked them deep in his heart.

Somehow, much to his surprise, he managed to find his car and got in. He was about to start the engine when his gaze fell on the colorful mums that blossomed along Prickett's driveway. They, along with the vast neat, trimmed grass, the huge, shade trees, all thrived with life. What right did they have to live when Diana was dead?

Dan retrieved his cell phone and his thoughts strayed to Debbie, not Linda. He felt both somewhat ashamed and amazed. A moment like this should be shared with his wife, not Debbie. Yet, it was Debbie he sought in his mind.

Guilt ate at him as he realized that he was finally free to release his grasp on his dead wife. Linda had Diana. Together, they played in a heaven filled with flowers and laughter. Together. But he was alone.

So alone.

He punched in Debbie's number.

* * *

The instant Debbie heard Dan's voice, she knew. "Come over, sweetheart, I'll be waiting for you."

Debbie opened her door as Dan got off the elevator. When he stepped into her suite, she opened her arms to him. Neither of them said a word. She prayed her love for him would provide the strength he so desperately needed.

Debbie had never seen Dan look worse. His face pale, his vacant eyes revealed the pent-up anger and anguish he had to be feeling. She wished he'd release his emotions, but instead he stood with his head buried in her shoulder. His body shook, but he wouldn't cry.

She led him to the bedroom, and he didn't complain when she removed his shoes. He lay on the bed, staring at the ceiling as though he could see past the roof and on toward heaven.

Debbie removed her own shoes and lay beside him, her head on his shoulder. Dan wrapped his arm around her. She moved in closer, hoping her body would give Dan the warmth he lacked.

They lay like that for a long time before Debbie ventured to whisper, "Tell me about it." Debbie stroked his cheek.

Still, Dan remained quiet, and Debbie wondered if she'd ever be able to penetrate the wall he had built around himself.

"Her. . .heart. . .failed." His voice was so soft, Debbie had to strain in order to hear him. "She was only four, and her heart failed. It was an old woman's heart, the doctor had said. How could that be? My parents were killed in a car accident when they were both in their sixties. Both were in perfect health. Linda's parents are still alive. Why did Diana's heart fail?"

"I don't know. Sometimes things happen that we don't like." Debbie recalled her own unhappy childhood. "But somehow we keep going."

"I don't want. . .to keep going."

"Oh, yes you do!" She threw both of her arms around him and held him as tight as she could.

He turned toward her, and his body shook with unconstrained spasms. This was followed by an audible sigh that almost didn't sound human. And that's when he cried.

Debbie knew he had come seeking comfort, and she did her best to provide it. She held him. She kissed him. She cried with him. The long hours finally gave way to exhaustion, and Dan eased off to sleep.

And still his body trembled even as he slept.

Chapter 26

At breakfast, Dan pushed his eggs around his plate. "I need to notify Linda's parents." He raked his hair with his fingers. "I don't know if I'm ready for that. I guess I should visit Diana's gravesite before I call them." He set the fork down. "And Bronson. I need to tell Bronson and Sylvia. She'd like to know, too. I just don't know if I'm ready to make those calls."

Debbie stood up. "I'll call Bronson and tell him to tell Sylvia."

Dan handed her Bronson's card. "I'm going back to my place to clean up. I'll come back and get you, then we'll go to the cemetery."

He stood up and Debbie noticed he hadn't eaten a thing.

"Want to hear something really stupid?"

Debbie waited for him to speak.

"I was thinking I should wear a suit. Diana would know I dressed up for her. Then I said 'no,' too formal. She'd want me to play with her, so I should wear jeans and a plain shirt. But it doesn't really matter, does it?"

"Diana will be glad you went to visit her. That's all that will matter to her."

"A teddy bear. I want to buy her flowers and a teddy bear. Will you help me choose them?"

Debbie nodded. "Of course."

* * *

Dan sat in the car, his gaze focused on the gravestone that should have read Diana Ann Springer. Instead it read Lydia Lynn Watson. He looked at Debbie who sat in the passenger seat, and he flashed her a smile he didn't quite feel.

He stepped out of the car and headed toward the grave. "Hello, sweetheart. It's me. Daddy. Daddy's here." He bent down and placed the teddy bear and flowers against the tombstone.

* * *

Debbie leaned against the car. She watched Dan lovingly arrange the flowers and teddy bear on Diana's grave. He sat by her grave, stroking the grass. She could hear him talk, but she couldn't make out the words.

At long last, he stood up and threw his daughter a kiss. He signaled for Debbie to come to him. "I told her all about you. I want you to meet her." He held out his hand for her to join him.

Hand-in-hand, they stood in front of the grave. "This is Debbie. Didn't I tell you she was pretty?"

"Hello, Diana. I've heard so much about you." Debbie felt foolish talking to a tombstone, but she knew it was important to Dan.

They stood for a while, then they turned back toward the car, and that's when she saw a man, leaning against a tree, studying them.

Chapter 27

Finding the cemetery proved to be a bit of a hassle. The cashier at the casino had not given Bronson very good directions. The more he talked to people, the more he came to realize that giving proper directions had become a lost art.

When he reached Glades Memorial, Bronson could see Dan and Debbie, both with their heads bowed, standing by a grave. He didn't want to interrupt so he quietly slipped out of his car and leaned against a tree.

When they started to head toward their car, Bronson approached them. He shook Dan's hand and thought how fragile he looked.

"Nice of you to come." Dan's voice sounded small and far away. "This is Debbie Gunther. Debbie, Detective Bronson."

Bronson offered her his hand. "Ma'am. My Carol and I—we caught your show a couple of nights ago. That was one heck of a good show. My Carol—she's going to be plenty jealous that I met you and she didn't."

"Thank you, Detective Bronson. Maybe later on, Dan can arrange for me to meet your wife."

"Yeah? Why my Carol would be just tickled pink." His smile faded as he turned to Dan. "I'm sorry for your loss."

Dan nodded. "Me, too. But I'll always be grateful to you."

"Don't mention it. Now, if you don't mind, I'll go visit with Diana for a few minutes."

He waited until Dan drove off before kneeling down at the grave. He removed the teddy bear and flowers Dan had placed and studied the area where the tombstone met the earth.

* * *

Dan tapped the steering wheel and slowly nodded. "I think it's time that you meet Linda. Are you up to it?"

Debbie felt as if an electric bolt ran through her body. Was Dan finally ready to accept the past? "Yes."

Dan flashed her a small smile and squeezed her hand. He remained quiet as he drove down Eastern Avenue. Debbie imagined that his thoughts were not with her, but with Linda and Diana.

He turned into King Tears Cemetery and parked under the shade of a large tree. "That's Linda's place." He pointed to his left.

At the foot of the tombstone, someone had recently placed a bouquet of bright red carnations and soft, pink mums. Debbie felt a stab of jealously when she realized that even though Linda had been dead for almost seven years, Dan still carried her memory in his heart. Then she felt shame for having been jealous. "That's a beautiful bouquet."

"Carnations and mums are—uh, were—Linda's favorite flowers. I come here once or twice a month and fill her in on what's going on in my life. She knows all about you—and she approves."

"I'm glad."

"Me, too." Dan reached for the door handle but didn't open the door. "You want to hear something dumb?"

Debbie nodded.

"When I come here to talk to Linda, it's almost as if she's there, listening to me. Today, when I went to visit. . ." He stopped, swallowed hard, and continued, "When I went to visit Diana, I didn't feel her there. I wanted her to be there, like Linda is, but Diana's grave was
. . .cold."

Debbie reached out and patted his upper arm. "You haven't adjusted to the idea, yet. Give it time."

"You're probably right. That must be it. Now come, let me introduce you to Linda. I've been promising her this meeting for quite a while."

* * *

Carol pushed her dessert plate away, reached for the cloth napkin, and wiped the edges of her mouth. She set the napkin down and looked at her husband. "Okay, out with it."

Bronson folded his arms in front of him and studied her. She still reminded him of the youthful, trim girl he had married. The years had been good to her. Although three years ago she had reached the magical age of fifty and had acquired some laugh lines at the edges of her eyes, she still looked good. The extra pounds she carried enhanced her appearance and made her that much more loveable. He flashed her what he hoped seemed like an innocent look. "Out with what?"

"This was a delicious dinner."

"Yes, ma'am, I agree."

"Expensive, too."

Bronson shrugged. "Haven't gotten the bill yet, but probably so."

"You're wearing dress pants and a nice shirt."

"You noticed?"

"Harry Bronson, we've been married for thirty-three years—"

"—and they've been glorious years."

She smiled, causing her eyes to twinkle. "Enough. What is it that you want?"

Bronson screwed up his face and made a noise like he was clearing his throat. "Can't a man take his beautiful wife of thirty-three married years out to a nice, fancy restaurant without her gettin' suspicious?"

"Not if his name happens to be Harry Bronson."

Bronson sighed. "If you knew all along I was up to somethin', why did you let me bring you to this place?"

"Because that's the only way I'll ever get you to take me to a nice, fancy restaurant—as you call it."

"Oh."

"So out with it."

"I need to work."

"Whaaat? We're on vacation, for Pete's sake. We're going back to Dallas?"

"No, I'm workin' here." Unable to meet her gaze, he looked down at the empty coffee cup and wished the waitress had stopped by with another refill. "All this time that you've been playin' Keno, I haven't been sittin' by the pool or up in the room restin' like you thought I was. I've been workin', sort of." He told her about meeting Dan, and how he had finally found his daughter. "I went to the cemetery today, and after Dan and Debbie left, I noticed somethin' that makes me want to go back before it gets dark."

Carol sighed, placed her hands on her cheeks, stared at her husband, and shook her head. "What am I going to do with you?"

Bronson gave her a fake smile.

Chapter 28

Surveillance.

Most detectives hated it. Not Bronson. It gave him time to think. Create. Some day he planned to write the all-American novel based on his cases. So far during the thirty-five years that he'd been on the force, he'd written the first three chapters.

Not on paper, of course. All in his mind. Problem was, he hated grammar and probably wasn't any good at it. But it would be a good novel. Maybe his hero would be illiterate. That would solve the problem. He could—

Bronson sat upright.

The gardener—groundskeeper—whatever he was called—had arrived.

It wasn't often Bronson got this lucky. He watched as the groundskeeper moved from grave to grave, discarding wilted flowers or picking up trash. Bronson waited until the man approached the area where Diana was buried.

Bronson strolled toward the plot next to Diana's resting-place and read the name on the tombstone: Shelly Walker. He watched as the groundskeeper bent down, his back toward Bronson.

Bronson grasped the opportunity to empty the contents out of his pocket. He dropped a wadded piece of paper, an empty cigarette box, and a plastic bag on the ground. He clasped his hands in front of him, bowed his head, and looked at Shelly's grave. His mind focused on the groundskeeper's movements.

Somewhere out in the street, a car honked and tires squealed. People drove so recklessly nowadays. That's why he hated driving.

The groundskeeper saw the trash lying by Bronson's feet and headed toward him. He picked up the plastic bag.

"Good evenin'." Bronson smiled at the man. He was much older than Bronson had originally thought. Age had bent him, like a weathered tree.

The old man mumbled something that Bronson did not understand.

"Thanks for keeping these grounds looking so nice."

The old man's head swiveled toward him. He looked at Bronson through rheumy eyes. "First time anybody's thanked me. Thought nobody noticed."

"I noticed, and I'm sure many others have too."

The old man gave him a curt nod. "Well, you're welcome." He picked up the discarded cigarette box and tossed it in the trash bag he carried.

"My Shelly appreciates it, too."

"Huh?"

Bronson pointed to the tombstone. "Shelly. I come visit her all the time."

"Never seen you before."

"No, I suppose not. I come mainly during the day. Maybe that's why we missed each other. But not much gets past me. You know what I mean?"

"No."

"Take this tombstone." Bronson pointed at Diana's grave.

"What 'bout it?"

"It's new, isn't it?"

"What if it is?"

"Then my interest is piqued. I'm a very curious person, and I hate to have my curiosity unanswered." Bronson reached into his pocket and took out a wad of money. He peeled off a ten. "How recent is this gravestone?"

Sharp, beady eyes stared at the money.

Bronson peeled off another ten.

What Others Know

The old man wet his dry, cracked lips.

"How old did you say it was?" Bronson handed the groundskeeper the money.

The old man grabbed the money with the speed of a striking cobra. "Don't rightly remember. Old age, you know, but it certainly was no more than a week or so."

"And before this tombstone was placed here, what did the previous one read?" Bronson fanned his money, just in case.

"Is that a twenty I see?"

"Could be."

The old man smacked his lips. "A gray-haired-old lady used to come visit this particular grave site. She's either a real dark Mexican or she's a light Black, not sure which." He pointed to the grave. "She said that was her husband of sixty-one years. She wished she could join him because she had no one left. No friends, no relatives. Nobody."

Bronson handed him the twenty. "Another twenty says you remember the name on the tombstone."

"That, I do. It read Edward 'Eddie' Barker, and since you're being so generous with your money for another ten I could force myself to remember the old woman's name."

"You drive a hard bargain." Bronson gave him the ten.

"Lakeyshia."

Bronson made a note and scanned the area. They were alone, not that he expected otherwise, but being careful is what had kept him alive all of these years. "Since you've been so generous with the information, I'll give you some free advice."

The old man tensed, but said nothing.

"If certain people knew you knew what you know..." Bronson paused, trying to figure out if that's what he meant to say. He figured that had to be right. "These people wouldn't hesitate to kill you to keep you quiet. My advice is be like the monkey: you see nothin', you hear nothin', you speak nothin', and while we're at it, let's throw an extra monkey in there. You know nothin'—you especially know nothin'." Bronson handed him another twenty. "That's for your trouble."

He bent down, picked up the wadded piece of paper and placed it in the old man's bag of trash. "Take care of yourself." He headed toward his car and whispered a small prayer. He certainly hoped that he hadn't put the old man's life in danger.

Chapter 29

A vast, hollow feeling gripped Dan as he executed a left turn into Glades Memorial. From the car, he could see the teddy bear and flowers he had placed on Diana's grave. He parked the car, took a deep breath, and headed toward it.

Hi, sweetheart. I didn't bring you anything today, just a heart filled with love and pain. Dan sat down in front of the tombstone and stroked the rubbery grass. *I miss you. I never had you, but I miss you. Dumb, huh?*

Dan looked up, past the grave, and saw a familiar figure heading toward him.

Bronson. What did he want? Anger nipped at Dan's nerves for the man's intrusion on this very private moment.

Dan looked behind him and noticed Bronson's car parked next to his. The detective must have made a wide arch in order to approach him from the front. Dan stood up.

"Debbie told me you were here. Hope you don't mind."

He did mind. He wanted to spend this time with Diana. He thought Debbie had known that. "I was just—"

"I know, but you'll want to hear what I have to say. Sylvia is already at Denny's waitin' for us. She's on her lunch break."

Dan looked at his watch. "At ten in the morning?"

"So, okay, maybe it's breakfast."

Dan looked at him.

"Brunch?"

Dan smiled, silently whispered a see you later to Diana, and walked with Bronson toward the cars.

"We'll take my car but you drive." Bronson fished the car keys out of his pocket and tossed them to Dan. "I'll bring you back when we're finished. Then, if you still want to, you can visit with Diana."

Why wouldn't he want to? What was Bronson up to? Dan nodded.

The ten-minute ride to Denny's was filled with an electric charge that warned Dan that this would be an important meeting. Maybe Bronson wanted to tell him that the world was ending. Or maybe beginning. Maybe he just wanted to buy him lunch. "So what gives?"

"It's rather complicated. That's why I invited Sylvia to join us. You do remember Sylvia, my niece, don't you?"

"Yes, of course. Does this have to do with the break-in at my apartment?"

"No, not really."

Dan looked out the window. If he could get away with strangling Bronson, he would.

By the time they reached Denny's parking lot, Dan had conjured several scenarios, but none came close to what he would hear.

Chapter 30

As they entered Denny's, Dan immediately spotted Sylvia. She was dressed in her full police uniform. She waved them over. As soon as they sat down, the waitress joined them.

Bronson ordered coffee and asked the waitress to keep a close eye on his cup because he didn't like to run out. Dan opted for a Sprite while Sylvia ordered eggs over-easy, bacon well done. After the waitress left, Dan turned to the others. "So, is this about Elko Bloomer and Joe Watson's deaths?"

"Not exactly." Bronson glanced at Sylvia, then down at the table.

"What then?"

Sylvia leaned forward. "My uncle has been working overtime. He did a bit of investigating yesterday."

Dan listened intently as he was very curious as to what Sylvia was going to tell him. He felt almost grateful to be experiencing a different emotion other than sorrow. "What kind of investigating?"

"I looked at your daughter's grave--"

The waitress set down a steaming cup of coffee and two containers of cream in front of Bronson. He asked for another tub of cream. She set two more down and said, "I'll be back with your drinks." She turned and left.

"And?" Dan heard his voice, coarse and dry.

Bronson's gaze met Dan's. "I just happened to glance at the place where the tombstone meets the earth, and guess what I noticed?"

The last thing Dan wanted to do was play guessing games. "What?"

"There's dirt."

Of course there was dirt. This is Vegas. Dan stared at Bronson. If he stared at him long enough, Bronson might get to the point faster.

"Almost three years have passed since your daughter...your daughter...uh—." Bronson poured four heaping spoons full of sugar into his coffee. "By now, I would tend to think the grass—"

"Jesus!" Dan almost jumped out of his seat. The customers around him turned to stare at him. He settled back down. "Are you trying to tell me that Diana might not be buried there?"

"My thoughts exactly. So I followed up. I met with a very reliable source last night." Bronson stirred his coffee and looked up at Dan.

Dan's heart skipped a beat. "And he said?"

"He said that an elderly black woman by the name of Lakeyshia Barker used to visit that gravesite. Used to go there almost daily, but it's been a couple of weeks now since she stopped comin'."

"Who is she?"

"As I said, she is an old lady who went to talk to her eighty-two year old husband. He's buried there."

Relief. Anger. Disbelief. Dan didn't know which emotion to grasp. "That means that Diana could be alive or buried somewhere else. It doesn't make much sense. Why the elaborate lie?"

"It's rather obvious, isn't it? Derek wanted you to think that Diana was dead. This way, you'd stop lookin' for her. Or maybe Derek is protectin' whoever has Diana. Now, it could be that Diana is dead, but for some reason or the other, they want to keep her gravesite a secret."

"She's alive. That's the only thing that makes sense." What a fool he'd been. He had accepted Derek's story at face value. Maybe he had done so because Derek had sounded so convincing. He wondered if he was an actor.

The waitress delivered the drinks and the meal. Sylvia reached out and patted Dan's shoulder. Dan looked up. He hadn't realized he'd covered his face with his hands. He waited until the waitress left, before speaking. "This puts me back where I was when I first started. All I have is dead ends."

"Not quite." Sylvia mixed part of her scrambled eggs and hash browns together. "You've got to put on a new hat. Think like a cop. Sort through all the information you have and follow each lead, no matter how small."

Bronson's grin couldn't possibly be wider. "That's my niece. She'll make a fine detective some day." He raised his coffee as in a toast.

Sylvia blushed and tried to hold back a smile.

Bronson reached into his pocket and produced a folded yellow notepad and a pen. He handed both to Dan.

Dan unfolded the paper. It was blank. What was he supposed to do with this? His gaze met Bronson's.

"That's just my style, maybe." Bronson signaled for the waitress to refill his coffee. "I start with a clean piece of paper. I jot down everythin' I know and see where it leads. I check 'em off as I finish followin' each notation and add details as I go along. Often, these new bits of information lead me to different trails that eventually solve the case."

Dan cleared off a space on the table and clicked the pen.

"Before you do that," Bronson said, "I need to tell you something important."

Chapter 31

Stuart Grimes parked his Camaro next to Dan's Honda. He sat in the car for a full ten minutes as he watched two middle-aged women place flowers on a grave. Stuart looked at his watch and wished they would hurry up and leave.

One of the women put her arm around the other one. They leaned toward each other, then headed for their car.

Good. Soon, Stuart would have the cemetery all to himself. He watched the women drive away. No one else was around. The moment the woman's car turned into the street, Stuart grabbed the bat he had brought with him and headed for Dan's car. Taking the stance of a professional baseball player ready to score his first homerun, Stuart swung the bat as hard as he could.

Dan's front windshield shattered, scattering bits of glass everywhere. The shards sparkled like brilliant diamonds as they caught the sun's rays. Stuart moved to his right and shattered the front side window. Next came the back window and finally, the window on the passenger's side.

Stuart stepped back and admired his handy work. He felt as pleased as a father watching his son take his first steps.

Stuart ran back to his car, threw the bat in the back seat, and once again headed for Dan's car. As he reached into his pants pocket, he glanced around. Lady Luck remained with him.

He was still alone in the cemetery. Stuart smiled at the clichés that popped into his mind. The cemetery was as quiet as death—not a soul stirred.

He snapped open the eight-inch blade and slashed Dan's front tires. He moved to the back. He had just finished doing the third one when a blue compact car turned into the cemetery.

Damn. No time to finish the job. Stuart closed the switchblade and stuffed it back into his pocket. He watched the car turn and head toward the other end of the cemetery.

Good.

From his shirt pocket, he retrieved the carefully folded hand-written note and Scotch tape. He taped the note to the steering wheel.

A young couple with a toddler trailing behind them got out of the car and headed toward a recently dug grave. The husband wrapped his arm around his wife.

Stuart figured that they hadn't even noticed he was there. Feeling a bit bold, he retrieved his switchblade, snapped it open, and finished Dan's tires with one quick slash.

He whistled softly as he headed back to his car.

Chapter 32

"Shit! What the hell is this!" Dan stared in disbelief at the damage to his car.

Bronson walked around the car, surveying the damage. "I reckon someone doesn't like you."

Ah, Bronson. The master of understatements. Dan's anger boiled too strongly to feel amused.

Bronson stopped by the passenger window and glanced in. "Seems you're in luck. Your vandalizer seems to have left his signature card."

"Meaning?"

"There's a note taped to your steering wheel."

Dan grabbed the note. His blood chilled as he read the typed note: "A major inconvenience, I'm sure, but cars can be mended. Do you suppose Debbie could heal as easily?"

Dan grabbed his cell phone, but before he could dial Debbie's number, his phone rang. The caller I.D. told him that the call came from an anonymous source. "Yes?"

"I enjoyed trashing your car, but you don't look too pleased with my handy work."

Dan scanned the area for the caller. The son-of-a-bitch who did this was watching him, he was sure.

Bronson pointed to a parked Camaro across the street. Even though it looked empty, Bronson headed that way.

"If you so much as touch one hair on Debbie's—"

"I have a message for you." Stuart's voice vibrated with menace. "Debbie is fine, but three days from now she won't be. Barbara Bloomer wrote that note I taped to your steering wheel. She also gave me a message to pass on to you. I'll read what she wrote: 'Mr. Springer, I am very disappointed that today's paper didn't carry an exposé on Prickett. I want my father's death avenged and it will be done within three days. Is that clear?'"

The line went dead.

Stuart sat up, and Dan watched him drive his Camaro away. Bronson ran out into the street, but was unable to get the license plate number.

"Barbara Bloomer is behind this," Dan said once Bronson returned to his side. "She's giving me three days to prove Prickett set off that bomb that killed her father. If I don't do something in those three days, Barbara has threatened to harm Debbie."

"Seems we have two choices here." Bronson raised his index finger. "One, we contact the police. Get her twenty-four hour security."

"And two?"

Bronson raised another finger. "You meet the deadline. In three days we expose Prickett."

"What would you do?"

"Both."

"I'm not sure getting the police involved at this time is particularly wise. The Vegas Mafia is very powerful."

"I was thinkin' of Sylvia. She's police, and I'm sure she's got friends who owe her maybe a favor or two?"

Dan liked that. Debbie could use the protection, and he'd be free to move around, expose Prickett, and find Diana.

If she was alive.

Chapter 33

When Debbie opened the door to her suite, Dan threw his arms around her and kissed her long and vehemently.

Debbie responded with a fervor of her own. "Wow! Oh, wow. Why the sudden passion?"

"I'm just happy to see you." He kissed her again. He couldn't stop kissing her. "You're safe."

"Of course, I'm safe. Why shouldn't I be?" She searched his eyes. Dan felt her muscles tense. "Tell me why I shouldn't be."

"Can I come in first?"

Debbie pulled him in, closed the door, and led him to the couch. "Speak."

Dan told her how he met with Bronson, then Bronson took him back to his car only to find it vandalized. When he mentioned the note, he wrapped her in his arms. He could feel her trembling. "This is what I wanted to avoid. If anything happens to you—"

Debbie pushed away from the embrace. "Listen to me, Dan. Nothing is going to happen to me, and if it does, remember that this was my decision. You pushed me away, and I refused to budge. I want to help you. Tell me what to do."

Dan smiled and stroked her cheek. "Somehow I knew that would be your answer. I told Bronson and Sylvia to come on up. They should be here any minute now."

Debbie wiggled her eyebrows and smiled mischievously. "In the meantime, let's make out."

"What?"

Debbie threw herself toward Dan. He caught her and kissed her.

A knock on the door interrupted them. "Damn, why must Bronson always be so punctual?"

Debbie giggled and untangled herself from Dan. She swung the door open. "Hello, Bronson, it's good to see you again." She shook his hand and looked at the woman standing behind him. "And you must be Sylvia Ulan."

Sylvia nodded and touched the shoulder of the man standing beside her. "This is my main squeeze, Anthony Sanchez."

Debbie and Anthony shook hands.

"Like Sylvia, I'm also a police officer," he said.

"Before we get started with this pow-wow, Debbie, ma'am, I want to caution you." Bronson hit his forehead with his opened palm as though he had forgotten something. "You know, Ms. Debbie, ma'am, if my Carol knew I was here again, talkin' to you, she would just kill me. I promised her I'd bring her by the next time, and here I am without her. I'd say she's probably your biggest fan."

Debbie smiled and winked as Colette would have done. "We'll just have to make arrangements for her to come visit."

"Yeah? We can do that?" Bronson's face beamed. "She'll be glad to hear that, but back to business. I have a request."

"And what's that?"

Bronson's eyes pierced Debbie's. "From now on, ma'am, don't open the door until you know who's on the other side. You got a peephole, use it every time. Now my niece here, Sylvia, and her guy—they're good police people, but you've got to do your share. Don't make it easy for someone to grab you."

Debbie nodded. "You're absolutely right. I've got to proceed with caution. It may be hard at first to think safety, but I'm a fast learner. Believe me, Detective Bronson, I have every intention of staying safe."

"That's what I wanted to hear." Bronson turned to Dan. "Let's get the ball rollin'."

They sat around the dining room table. Debbie made coffee for Bronson, poured a large glass of orange juice for herself, and Cokes for everyone else.

Dan unfolded the yellow notepad paper Bronson had given him at Denny's. It was now filled with notes. "While waiting at the car rental place, Bronson and I mapped out a few things. Here's what we came up with."

"Anthony, Sylvia, between the two of you, you'll be providing Debbie with twenty-four hour security for at least the next three days."

Sylvia nodded. "No problem. Both Anthony and I have requested some personal time off. We won't leave Debbie's side, and we'll take shifts sleeping. Both of us will be in civilian clothes, so no one will label us as police."

Debbie sipped her juice. "That sounds good, but how do I explain your twenty-four hours a day presence?"

Sylvia and Anthony exchanged looks. "As of now, Anthony and I are your friends from Hollywood. We're here visiting you."

"That'll work," Dan said.

Sylvia reached for her soda, gulped some down, and nodded. "I think so, too."

Dan placed a check mark by the notation that read Provide for Debbie's safety. He studied the notes momentarily before continuing. "At Denny's, Bronson, Sylvia, and I discussed Pam Banis, your so-called school friend and hair dresser. We felt it was too convenient for her to show up at this time and have connections with both Barbara Bloomer and Melody Prickett. She's working, we're sure, for one side or the other and possibly using you to get information about me. Play her game. Don't let her know we're wise to her. Turn the circumstances around and see what information you can get from her. Anthony and Sylvia will be with you. They're trained professionals, so they'll be able to guide you."

Dan reached out and wrapped his hand around Debbie's. "But above all, be safe. If things start getting hot, promise me you'll walk away."

Debbie flashed him a tiny smile and nodded.

The knot in Dan's stomach tightened a bit more. Debbie would never let go. At least she had Anthony and Sylvia to watch over her for now. But he had to work fast.

Dan turned back to his notes, then looked back up. "Bronson has volunteered to follow up on Derek Watson. At this point, we're not sure if he is Diana's father, as he claims." He cleared his throat, trying to get rid of the distaste the sound of the word *father* associated with name Derek Watson produced.

"As for me, I'm going to follow up on Lakeyshia Barker. Her husband Eddie is buried in the grave that's supposed to be my daughter's. Someone must have paid her a nice lump of money to allow her husband's tombstone to be replaced with . . . Diana's." He folded the yellow notepad paper and returned it to his pocket. "Any questions?"

Blank eyes stared back at him. "In that case, I want to reiterate what Bronson told me at Denny's. Right before I started making the list, he told me to stop and think about this. We're not playing Cowboys and Indians here."

"Nor cops and robbers." Bronson emptied his cup and motioned for Debbie to refill it. He reached out for the sugar bowl.

Dan waited until Debbie returned with Bronson's steaming cup of coffee before continuing, "This is not a game. We could get hurt. If any of you want to back out, now's the time. No hard feelings."

"None of us are going to back out." Sylvia looked at everyone around the table for confirmation. "We're a team, then."

Dan stood up. "Okay, that's all for today. We will meet tomorrow to catch each other up on our findings."

Bronson turned to Dan. "Speaking of findin', did you tell Debbie what we did?"

"What did we do?" Then he remembered, "Oh, I'd forgot. Debbie, Bronson and I were concerned about your safety so we put listening devices in your suite."

"Listening devices?" Debbie stared at Dan, then at Bronson.

"Only one who can listen in is me," Bronson said. "Haven't done it yet. Wanted to get your permission before I listened."

"If someone comes in here and somehow manages to overpower us," Sylvia said, "it would be beneficial."

Debbie shook her head. "It would have been nice if you had asked me before you did it. Jesus. I'm not crazy about you listening in on me. I don't get much privacy as it is. Now I'll have none at all."

"I'm so sorry, ma'am. I should have asked you first—"

Debbie took a deep breath. "It's okay. This is all kind of stressing me out. I guess it can't hurt."

"Good. It will make us feel better if we can listen in and know that you're okay," Bronson said. "Oh, one other thing. I'll need you to promise not to turn on the TV nor the radio. If you do, then I won't be able to hear."

"Right. No TV. No radio." Debbie stood up and headed for the phone. "I'll begin by setting up an appointment with my hairdresser, my dear, childhood friend, none other than Pam Banis."

Chapter 34

Dan slammed the phone down. The manager at the Honda dealership told him his car wouldn't be ready for at least seven more days. He called Avis and told them he wouldn't be returning the Ford Focus he had rented at least until Saturday.

He headed for the kitchen, poured himself a large glass of ice-cold lemonade, and grabbed the telephone book. He didn't hold much hope for finding Lakeyshia Barker there, but still he tried. As he had expected, there were several Barkers listed, but no Lakeyshias.

He tried the first Barker. The woman who answered had never heard of a Lakeyshia Barker. The second number was no longer a working number. A grumpy man answered the third call. "No Lakeyshias live here. Next time, check your numbers before calling." He hung up.

Dan's luck didn't change with the remainder of the calls. He sat at his dining room table, tapping his fingers, trying to think like a policeman. His gaze rested on the stack of bills he needed to pay. The one on top was the electric bill. "Of course," he said. He would pay Ivy a visit at the Electric Company. For the past several years, whenever Dan needed something that involved getting information from the Electric Company, he always turned to Ivy. And why shouldn't he? She was, after all, his cousin.

He slammed the phone book shut, grabbed his car keys, and headed out. A few minutes later, he was back inside his apartment. He had grabbed his own car keys instead of the ones for the white Focus.

It took him a little more than half-an-hour to reach the Electric Company.

"Next," Ivy said.

That would have been Dan, but he stepped back and allowed the person behind him, a young mother with two toddlers and a crying baby, to go in front of him. She looked at him gratefully and mouthed a "Thank you."

"Next."

This time Dan stepped up to the window.

Ivy, a matronly looking woman with long, stringy hair and big, round glasses, smiled and looked up at Dan. Her smile faded. "Oh no, not you. Please tell me you're here to pay your electric bill."

"You know that was rather dumb of me. I left it at home."

"I assumed as much. So what is it that you want this time?"

Dan feigned a hurt look. "Do I really need a reason to come visit my favorite cousin? Am I that bad? Do I come see you only when I need something?"

"Yes to all three questions."

"Okay, how 'bout I take you to lunch as a way of saying thanks for all you've done?"

Ivy stiffened. "Now I know you really want something." She sighed. "I'll do it. You don't need to pay me."

"I know, but I would really like to take you to lunch."

She arched her eyebrows in surprise. "How about next week?"

"Next week sounds great. How 'bout I stop by at noon next Tuesday?"

"Sure." She smiled. "Now that you've completely charmed me, what do you really want?"

He lowered his voice and leaned toward the window. "I want the address of one of your customers."

"And what else?"

"That's all, just the address."

"You're sure? The other times it's been a big long complicated research project."

"Not this time."

"I assume it's for official business."

"Strictly official."

"What's the name?"

"Lakeyshia Barker." He handed her a piece of paper. "I wrote her name down for you."

"How thoughtful." She grabbed the paper.

* * *

Lakeyshia lived in North Las Vegas in an area where, if the entire house was still standing, it was considered a luxury. Dan turned on 48th St. and followed the numbers to Lakeyshia's house. Weeds had overtaken most of the front yard. The few flowers along the edge of the walkway had wilted.

As he stepped onto the decaying wooden porch, Dan could hear the television blaring. At least someone was home.

He took another step and that's when the unmistakable smell hit him. One whiff of that sweet, yet pungent odor triggered a lost primal memory. Dan hesitated, wondering what he should do. He covered his nose and forced himself to move forward.

He noticed that the door was slightly open. Refusing to accept what his senses told him, he whispered, "Mrs. Barker?" He cleared his throat and repeated her name more forcefully.

The big screen TV characters spoke of betrayed love. "Mrs. Barker?" He wanted to run outside and swallow some fresh air. "My name is Dan Springer. I need to speak to you."

He stepped inside.

The scent of decay attacked his nostrils.

"I—Jesus!"

Lakeyshia Barker's unseeing eyes stared at the new television set. She had been tied to the chair so she wouldn't fall when the intruder shot her in the forehead.

Chapter 35

Hand in hand, Bronson and Carol strolled through Madame Tussaud's Wax Museum. Bronson liked the idea of the wax figures being out in the open instead of behind some invisible electrical line. His Carol posed with Elvis Presley and Brad Pitt. They laughed and giggled like high school students.

When they finished, they spent time at the curio shop, then leisurely headed back to their motel room. Carol splashed some water on her face and ran a brush through her hair. "I'd invite you to come play the Keno machines with me, but I know you'll tell me you're going swimming or some other silly thing, but what you're really going to do is go to work."

Bronson smiled. Dang, that woman could read him like a book. That was good. At least he wouldn't have to pretend to take a nap so he could sneak out and work as soon as she closed the door behind her.

Before checking on Derek Watson's whereabouts, he might as well check out the bugs in Debbie's suite to be sure that they worked. He knew Debbie was safe with Sylvia and Anthony, but it wouldn't hurt to check the system out anyway. You never know when it'd come in handy. He put the earphones on.

Carol kissed Bronson goodbye. "I'm only going to spend fifty dollars. When I run out, I'll come back up here and watch some TV, or I might go to the pool. See if I can find any studs down there."

Bronson swatted her bottom. Carol giggled and took off.

Bronson set his equipment on the small motel table. He turned on the receiver and picked up part of a conversation between Sylvia and Anthony. Good. It worked. He turned it off and removed the earphones.

He stood up, stopped, and sat back down. What had Anthony said? He turned it back on and listened.

". . .be bothering you. This is the third time you've mentioned it since we got here," Sylvia said.

"Is it really?" Anthony hesitated for a second, then continued, "Hell, yeah, it's bothering me. Ralph is my boss, and he's on the take. I hate crooked cops. I hate Ralph Simpson and all he stands for."

Bronson turned off the listening device.

He agreed with Anthony. Crooked cops turned his stomach.

* * *

Bronson removed his glasses and rubbed the bridge of his nose. He was parked across the street from the police station, staring at its parking lot. There was absolutely no reason in the world why he shouldn't get out, introduce himself, and explain to the policemen that he was looking for Derek Watson.

As a courtesy, the police would open their records to him or maybe even let him check the records himself. It was that simple.

But not really.

Something tugged at the pit of his stomach, and one thing he had learned from all those years he had put in as a detective was to listen to his inner voice. Right now it told him that Anthony was worried about Ralph Simpson. Now maybe this Simpson person had nothing to do with this case, but if Bronson stuck his nose in the police office, he might accidentally trigger something that would alert Simpson. What he really needed to do was talk to Anthony about Simpson.

But that of course was something that would have to be done at a later time. Right now, what Bronson had to do was to make up his mind if he should go into the police station or get his information elsewhere. He tapped the steering wheel and continued to stare at the parking lot. Maybe if he stared long enough, he would find the answer.

An unexpected knock on Bronson's car window caused him to jump. He rolled down the window and stared at a policeman's youthful face. His nametag identified him as K. Sante. "Can I help you, officer?"

"Let's see some I.D."

"Sure." Bronson retrieved his wallet. "I'm Harry Bronson, Dallas city police detective." He showed him his badge and I.D. card.

Sante studied the badge. "I'm Officer Sante. Mind telling me what you're doing parked across the street from the police station?"

"Ah, I see what this is about. Tends to look suspicious, huh?"

"You could say that."

"I did."

Sante frowned. "What?"

"Say that."

"Oh." Sante considered that for a minute. "What is it that you need, Detective Bronson?"

"Nothin', really. I reckon you could say that I'm a bit homesick. I promised the Mrs. a vacation, but I really enjoy work. Thought I might go in, introduce myself, but what's the purpose? If it's okay with you, I'll be headin' back to the motel."

Sante nodded and stepped away from the car. "You do that, and enjoy the rest of your vacation."

"Will do." Bronson pulled out. A block away, he turned into the parking lot of a strip mall, took out a city map, located the building he was looking for, and headed for the Clark County Records office.

* * *

"Evenin', ma'am," Bronson said once his turn came up. He flashed her his badge. "I'm Detective Bronson and I'm lookin' for a Derek Watson. Thought maybe you might help me locate him."

The young clerk's eyes lit up. "Oh, really? You want me to help you? I thought you guys had access to all sorts of records, even more than we do here."

Bronson looked around. He leaned over and whispered, "We do, but this is a sensitive matter, so we can't go traditional routes, if you know what I mean."

"Sure. Of course. You can count on me. What is it that you need exactly?"

"An address—or any kind of information you may have that will lead us to him."

"What did this guy do?"

Bronson made a face. "Like I said, it's a sensitive matter. I really can't discuss it. But we're closin' in on him, and when we do, I'll come back and fill you in."

"Yeah? Hey that's great. Now, what was that guy's name again?"

* * *

The clerk's search proved to be fruitless.

Derek Watson owned no property, paid no taxes, had no social security number, and no driver's license.

Simply put, Bronson reasoned, Derek Watson did not exist, at least in this county.

Chapter 36

Dan ran out of the house, gasping for air.

Had someone killed Lakeyshia just to keep her from talking to him about the tombstone? What kind of a sick bastard would prey on old people like that? Dan steadied himself and eyed the neighborhood to see if anybody had seen him. The street looked deserted.

Forcing himself to walk at a normal pace, Dan headed toward his rental car, climbed in, and drove away. He remembered seeing a convenience store maybe three or four miles down the road. He would use the store's pay phone to call 911.

Once there, he located the phone booth and punched in the numbers. When the dispatcher answered, Dan said, "An elderly woman by the name of Lakeyshia Barker was murdered. The address is 340 48th St."

"Who is—"

Dan cut him off. "That address is 340 48th St." He hung up. At a steady pace, he returned to the Focus and drove away.

As he left the northern section of Las Vegas, Dan found himself gasping for air. Not only did he feel responsible for Lakeyshia's death, he felt he was betraying her by deserting her.

He spotted a gasoline station and pulled over. He retrieved his cell phone and called Debbie. She answered on the second ring.

"Someone killed Lakeyshia Barker."

There was a pause, then, "I'm free for the next three hours. Where do you want to meet?"

"Somewhere where there's a crowd." He didn't want her to be alone and vulnerable. "How about at the main entrance to the Fashion Mall? The entrance facing The Strip."

"I'll be there in ten minutes."

"Make it twenty. It'll take me that long to get there." Dan hung up and was about to start the engine when his phone rang. He immediately thought of Debbie, but his caller I.D. simply read Call from Unknown. "Hello?"

"Dan? Bronson here. Do you know any artists?"

"What kind of artists?"

"One who specializes in drawing people."

Dan searched his mind. "Not off hand. Wait, I don't know him personally, but there's usually a guy at the mall who draws people."

"And the mall is. . ."

"The Fashion Mall."

"Can you meet me there?"

"As a matter of fact, I'm supposed to meet Debbie there in about twenty minutes."

"There?"

"Main entrance to the mall, facing The Strip."

"I'll be there, too."

Dan considered telling Bronson about Lakeyshia, but figured that could wait. He pulled away from the gasoline station and headed toward the mall.

* * *

Anyone seeing the Fashion Mall from the street would be deceived. Even though the mall occupies the entire block, the structure does not appear to be as big as it actually is. Only when the visitor steps inside, does he realize that this is a huge three level mall, for what it lacks in width, it makes up in length.

Dan approached the mall from the rear parking lot. He knew that if he parked in the underground section, the car would be in the shade. Chances were thought that the lots would be full, and he didn't feel like fighting with other drivers for a coveted, shaded parking space. He took the first available spot, locked the car, entered the mall, headed upstairs, and worked his way through the crowds and on to the main entrance.

He immediately spotted Anthony, Sylvia, and Debbie. Dan kissed Debbie, hugged Sylvia, and shook Anthony's hand. He had barely done that when Bronson arrived.

In an uncharacteristic gesture of warmth, Bronson wrapped his arm around his niece and kissed her forehead. "I imagine you two would appreciate a break. Me and Dan—we'll take good care of Debbie. Why don't you meet her back at her place in, say, two hours?"

Anthony and Sylvia nodded and smiled. "Only if you're sure," Sylvia said.

"I'm sure."

Sylvia squeezed Debbie's arm and they left. Dan reached for Debbie's hand and the three of them entered the mall. Debbie leaned toward Dan. "Are you all right?"

He nodded. "I'm better. We'll talk later." He turned to Bronson. "What's with the artist?"

"Hope I don't shock you when I tell you that Derek Watson doesn't exist."

"I'm shocked," Dan said.

Debbie stopped to look at a display in a store. Dan and Bronson waited outside.

"You look like shit," Bronson said.

"Thank you. It's one of my better looks."

"Want to talk about it?"

"Yes, but I've got to get myself together first. Give me time."

"It's yours."

Dan forced Lakeyshia out of his mind. He'd have to come to grips with that, but for now the best thing to do was change the subject. "You suppose Derek Watson is an alias?"

"Reckon so."

"So how are we going to find him?"

"You're the key. You've seen him. You can describe him, can't you?"

Dan nodded. That was one person he was never likely to forget.

"I thought as much. Way I figure is if I have a drawing of this Derek person, I can fax it back home to this young police officer I know by the name of Loyce Guthrie. Very sharp woman. I'm going to fax her the picture and any information you have and let's see what she can come up with. Now, let's hope your artist is not busy at this moment."

He wasn't.

Bronson told him what he wanted. "Think you can do it?"

The artist stroked his salt-and-pepper colored beard. His hair had been pulled back into a long ponytail that went past the middle of his back. Slowly, he nodded. "Yeah, sure. I can do that. Never done it before, but it sounds like fun."

It took the artist a bit over an hour to get a sketch out, but when he finished, Dan felt as though he were staring at Derek Watson's face.

"We've got a bit under an hour, before we need to get Debbie back to the casino for rehearsal." Bronson looked at his watch. "Why don't we get a cup of coffee? I want to know if you were successful in finding Lakeyshia."

Before they could move, a group of teens blocked their way as they gathered around Debbie. "Aren't you Colette?"

Debbie smiled and winked, as Colette would have done. "Actually, I'm Debbie Gunther, but on stage, I impersonate Colette."

"That's what we meant."

"I told you it was her."

"Can I have your autograph?"

"Yeah, me, too?"

Debbie signed five different sheets of paper and the teens took off, staring at the signature as though any minute it would turn to gold.

"That happen often?" Bronson eyed the departing, giggling teens.

"It's happening more and more often." Dan wrapped his arm around Debbie. "My gal is getting herself quite well-known."

"Sometimes that's good, and sometimes that's bad." She reached for Dan's hand. "Come on, let's get that cup of coffee."

The "cup of coffee" turned out to be a tall glass of orange juice for Debbie, a Coke for Dan, and coffee for Bronson. They shared a large sweet roll while Dan filled them in on Lakeyshia's death. Dan barely touched his Coke and neglected the sweet bread.

Bronson ate his share, then moved on and consumed the part that Dan should have eaten.

By the time Dan finished relating the story, he felt drained and miserable.

Debbie reached out and squeezed his hand. "I don't understand why you didn't wait for the police to show up."

"I was afraid that if I hung around and waited for them, somehow Derek would find out that I suspect he lied to me about Diana. I don't want that getting back to him."

"You did the right thing." Bronson took the last large piece from the roll and ate it. "That set my thinkin' wheels goin', and I'd like to go back to the very beginning. I know this is painful, but it's got to be done."

Dan frowned and Debbie squeezed his hand.

"You said Linda was killed because. . ."

"Those articles I was doing on the drugs."

"You sure about that?"

"Yeah. There were calls warning me to drop the series."

"But suppose the calls were a decoy?"

"Meaning?"

"Meaning their intent all along was to take Diana. It was never about drugs."

Dan felt the blood leave his face. For a minute he was numb. "And that's why Derek would lie. He doesn't want me finding Diana and claiming her back."

"Precisely."

"Which means Diana is still alive."

"Could be. Now don't get your hopes up. He might have been telling you the truth about that. We don't know. Let's just take this one step at a time."

Dan nodded, but no matter how hard he tried, he kept hoping Diana was alive.

Bronson leaned forward. "How sure are you that this Derek person is Diana's current father?"

"Pretty sure. If he's not the father, then he knows who her father is. The picture he showed me was definitely Diana." And he silently added, I'd recognize her anywhere.

Chapter 37

As soon as Debbie Gunther stepped into the Fashion Mall, Nick's phone started to ring. Amazing what people will do for money. When Debbie's and Dan's location was confirmed, Nick jumped into his car and sped off, heading toward the mall. He had not only been told about Debbie and Dan, but he also had been handed information on Dan's rental car. One enterprising informer had even recorded Dan's new license plate.

After pulling into the half-full lot, Nick drove up and down the aisles, looking for Dan's car. Once he thought he had found it, but it turned out to be a different Focus. Same off-white, but definitely not Dan's.

Four aisles further, he found the car. This time he was sure it belonged to Dan. He checked the license plate. It matched. Nick slowed down and looked around. The car right on the corner was pulling out.

What luck. He could park, sit and wait for Dan and Debbie. He reached under the car seat and felt the cool metallic touch of his gun.

From where he was he'd be able to get one clear shot and make his getaway in the confusion.

He knew one shot, one chance was all he had.
No problem.
He never missed.

* * *

"Debbie's got rehearsal coming up. Let's take her back and make sure Anthony and Sylvia are there. If not, we'll wait until they arrive, then we'll go to my office where we can fax

Loyce Guthrie the drawing and information." Dan fished the keys out of his pocket.

"Sounds like a plan." Bronson followed them.

"Where are you parked?"

"About two rows away from you. I saw your rental on the way in." Bronson scanned the lot as they walked toward the parked cars.

Dan held back a bit. "Anything wrong?" He glanced around the parking lot but didn't see anything unusual.

"Nah, that's just me. Always the detective. I expect trouble in every corner. Seldom get it, though, thank God." They turned down the row where Dan had parked the car.

"Personally, I think you guys are making too much out of this." Debbie smiled and shook her head, but Dan could see she was putting on a brave front.

They reached Dan's white Focus.

Dan was about to open the car's door when he saw Bronson's eyes widen. Time both froze and sped. He followed Bronson's gaze. He saw a man in a parked car, engine idling. He pointed something at them.

A gun.

Both Bronson and Dan dove toward Debbie in an attempt to knock her down.

As Dan flew through the air, he heard the hiss of an angry wasp close to his ear, as a single shot ripped the air. The car sped away.

Chapter 38

Pam opened her eyes and stared at the clock. It read 12:52. She couldn't believe she'd slept that late. Normally, she was up at 6:00 in the morning and by 6:30 she was cutting, trimming, tinting, or styling somebody's hair.

But not any more.

Pam had three customers: Melody Prickett, Barbara Bloomer, and Debbie Gunther. That was it, only three, and she made at least twice as much money as before.

She considered rolling over and sleeping some more, but what the heck, she'd already wasted half a day. Well, maybe not wasted. Every once in a while, she enjoyed sleeping late like this.

Her phone rang. Should she let it ring?

She reached for it. "Hello?"

"Pam? Irma, here. I've been calling and calling, but I haven't been able to reach you. Have you been out of town?"

Pam frowned. She shouldn't have answered.

"I definitely need my hair done, and you know you're the only one who I let touch my hair."

Pam closed her eyes and she could see Irma's hair. Short and wiry. Very hard to work with, and Irma always expected miracles. Pam would never have to do Irma's hair again. A rush of excitement filled Pam.

"I guess you haven't heard? I'm retired."

"Retired? That's preposterous. Why, you're only . . . well, you're young, aren't you?"

"Yes, of course, but nevertheless, I'm retired. Try another girl at the shop." Pam hung up and felt good. Nothing was going to spoil this day. She'd take a long, hot shower, then. . .

The phone rang again.

Pam glared at it. Maybe she shouldn't. The call should be good news. After all, she got to sleep in late. Then, she got to tell Irma off. What was it they say about threes? Good things come in threes. She grabbed the phone. "Hello?" She almost sang the word.

Silence.

"Hello?"

"We're going on with the plan."

The bottom fell out of Pam's world. No! This was supposed to be a wonderful day. "Why?"

"Are you questioning me?" came the harsh voice over the phone.

"No, of course not." The last thing she needed to do was to incur his wrath. "What exactly am I supposed to do?"

"You're doing Debbie's hair today at four."

How did he know? "Yes."

"Call her. Tell her you need to talk to her. Make some excuse to get her to your house. She's got two bodyguards. They'll want to come along. Let them. When they get to your house, let them in. We'll take care of the rest."

Chapter 39

Dan opened his eyes, glanced around, and saw numerous, unfamiliar faces staring at him. The smell of hot, dirty asphalt assaulted his nostrils. He was on the ground and his muscles ached. Why were these people looking at him? What did they want? What had happened? Where was he?

There had been a noise...

A noise? What kind of a noise?

A bullet. Oh, God, somebody had shot at them.

Perspiration, cold and clammy, beaded on Dan's forehead. *Debbie!*

She was under him. So was Bronson. Ignoring his aching muscles, Dan stood up and saw both Bronson and Debbie move. Even though Dan knew he should relax, the anxiety in his stomach tightened a notch. "Are you all right?"

"I'll be sore tomorrow." Bronson dusted himself off.

"The sooner you big lugs get off me, the sooner I'll be fine," Debbie said.

The sound of Debbie's voice helped Dan relax. He helped her up.

Bronson looked at her. "You're sure, ma'am, you're all right?"

Debbie, looking a bit pale, nodded. Her soft, frilly blouse was now more gray than white. Her pants had a tear below the right knee.

Bronson moved toward Dan and whispered only loud enough for Dan to hear. "Police will be here shortly. We can handle this in one of two ways: my way or your way. And before you ask, if we do it my way, then I tell the police everything, including Barbara Bloomer's threatening note to you."

"You do that and she'll never tell me who the informer is. I have to know that. Give me time. Please." Dan heard the wailing of a siren approaching.

"Then we do this your way."

"Which is?"

"Beats me." Bronson shrugged. "You do all the talkin'. I'm keepin' quiet."

"For once."

The mall police arrived, and the first thing they did was to help secure the area.

For all the good that'll do.

The Las Vegas police came next, followed by an ambulance.

Good grief.

* * *

From the time Debbie walked into her suite to the time she left, seventeen minutes had elapsed. She took a very quick shower, ran a brush through her hair, and bandaged her skinned knee. She also tended to Dan's bruised arm, and Bronson's cut forehead.

This made Debbie over an hour late for rehearsal. When she walked in, her director, Bill Davis, pointed to his watch and shook his head.

Debbie mouthed the word *sorry*, ran up to the stage, and picked up where the dancers were without missing a beat.

A sense of pride rushed through Dan. Debbie was a real trooper.

Bronson nudged him. "Let's go."

Dan's gaze bounced toward Debbie.

"She'll be fine," Bronson reassured him. "Sylvia and Anthony are here."

He knew that, but that didn't help. He and Bronson had been there when someone had shot at Debbie, and he knew exactly who that someone had been, in spite of his denial of knowledge when he talked to the police.

"I have no idea why he shot at us," Dan had told the policeman. "Maybe we were at the wrong place at the wrong time." Dan shrugged. "I couldn't even tell you what he looked like or what he drove."

The policeman had given him a knowing look and probably would have detained him longer had not Bronson and Debbie stuck by him.

That had made Dan feel like a con artist, a feeling he didn't care to have. He had lied to protect Barbara Bloomer. Yet, she had betrayed him, promised him that Debbie would be safe for three days. Anger rose within him. "I'm going to pay Barbara Bloomer a visit, and I'd like for you to come along."

"And why is that?" Bronson asked.

"So you can keep me from killing her."

"I can do that."

"What, kill her?"

Bronson smiled.

Chapter 40

Dan whipped out his cell phone and tossed it to Bronson. "Do me a favor. I don't like to use this thing while I'm driving. Please call Barbara for me. When the phone's ringing, give it back to me."

Bronson punched in the numbers and waited for it to ring. He handed it to Dan.

"I'm ten minutes away from your house," Dan said once Barbara had answered. "Call your guard and clear me and my friend." He didn't wait for an answer. He hung up.

Twelve minutes later, he turned into her driveway. When he reached the guard's gate, he slowed down, but did not stop. The guard, the same one Dan had beaten, shot him a dirty look and waved him on.

The maid led Dan and Bronson into the study. "I will notify Ms. Bloomer that you're here." She pointed to the couch. "Please make yourselves comfortable."

Dan crossed his arms and remained standing. He ignored the maid.

"As you wish." She stepped out into the hallway and closed the door behind her.

"Are we in an ugly mood?" Bronson asked.

Dan ignored him.

"I reckon that means yes." Bronson looked at the mahogany coffee table. An oversized picture book of Las Vegas rested on the table along with expensive looking knick-knacks. "I wonder if she has a pot of coffee on."

Dan frowned. "Coffee? You've got a serious coffee addiction, my friend."

"True, but it's my only vice," Bronson replied.

The door opened and Barbara stepped in. She looked stunning in a tight blue jump suit with its collar pulled up. Simple, yet elegant, silver jewelry complimented her outfit.

"Mr. Springer, I wish I could say that it's a pleasure to see you, but I still haven't quite forgiven you yet." She turned to Bronson. "And you're that policeman friend of his, aren't you?"

"You could say that. Name's Bronson, ma'am. Harry Bronson." He offered her his hand.

She accepted it. "Would any of you care for something to drink?"

"Coffee, ma'am. Coffee would be perfect."

Dan shook his head. "This isn't a social call."

"I didn't figure it was."

"Does this mean I don't get coffee?" Bronson asked.

Barbara looked at Bronson.

Dan looked at Bronson.

Bronson smiled.

Barbara smiled.

Dan didn't smile.

Barbara leaned forward and pushed the button on an intercom. "Please bring coffee for Mr. Bronson."

Barbara straightened up and turned to Dan. "So you're here to tell me you exposed Prickett and the story will break out in tomorrow's paper?"

"Only in your dreams."

Barbara stiffened and gave Dan a puzzled look.

"We're here about the betrayal."

"The betrayal?"

"You said three days."

"That's right. I gave you three days to expose Prickett. I gave you three days of safety, for you and Debbie."

"Then why was she shot at today?"

Barbara's genuine startled look told Dan everything he needed to know. "You didn't do it, did you?"

"No, I didn't. What—"

The door opened and the maid entered carrying a silver tray with a matching silver decanter. There was also a china plate filled with a variety of cookies and three matching china cups and saucers. The cream and sugar set matched the decanter. She set the tray down and walked backwards toward the door.

"Thank you, Erica."

The maid nodded, turned, and left.

"I am a woman of my word. I said three days, I meant three days." Barbara poured Bronson a cup of coffee and handed it to him. "Is Debbie all right?"

"The shooter missed. We're all a bit shaken, but okay." Dan watched as Bronson grabbed a cookie and gulped it down. "If you didn't order it, who did?"

"Prickett?" Barbara sat down and folded her legs. Her hands rested neatly on top of her knees. "Now you have another reason for going after Prickett."

"He's got no reason to harm Debbie."

Barbara stood up. "Apparently he does. All I know is that you only have two days left. I'd advise you to get to work."

"Words of wisdom." Dan stood up.

Bronson remained seated. "I haven't finished my coffee."

Barbara looked at Bronson.

Dan looked at Bronson.

Bronson drunk his coffee. "You said Prickett was maybe behind today's shooting. What, ma'am, would cause you to say that?"

Barbara shrugged. "First name that popped into my mind."

"And why's that?"

"I suppose it's because I hate that man. He had my father killed."

"Did he now?"

Barbara froze as though caught off guard. She quickly recuperated. "Yes, of course. We all know that."

"And we know this because. . ."

"I have my sources."

Bronson raised his eyebrows. "I bet you do." Bronson grabbed another cookie. "Think I'd like to talk to your maid. It's Erica, right?"

Barbara nodded. "Yes, that's correct. May I ask why you want to talk to her?"

"I'd like to get the recipe for this coffee. You see, my Carol, she's a wonderful woman, but she doesn't know how to make good coffee because she doesn't drink coffee herself. This is by far the best coffee I've had for quite sometime."

"I'll pass that on to Erica."

"I appreciate that, ma'am." He walked out and joined Dan who by now stood beside the car door.

"Do you still want to go to my office?" They got in and Dan drove off.

"Sure do. Got to send that information to Loyce. We need to track down Derek Watson. I'm sure he'll lead us to Diane." Bronson buckled his seat belt.

Dan stopped at a red light. Traffic, as usual, crawled along at a snail's pace. Congested traffic spared very few of Las Vegas's streets. "Life's ironical."

"You noticed."

"Nothing wrong with my observational powers."

"So why's life ironical?"

"Every place I turned, there was Derek. Gave me the creeps. Didn't want to see him. Now. . ." The light changed and Dan sped off at ten miles an hour.

"And now that we go lookin' for him, he's nowhere to be found."

"Exactly."

Bronson removed his glasses and cleaned them. He chewed on the earpiece. "Life's ironical."

"You noticed."

"Nothing wrong with my observational powers. In fact, I was just thinkin'. . ."

"Oh, oh. We're in trouble."

"Exactly."

"So what were you thinking?"

"Have you ever wondered why the shooter missed Debbie?" Bronson asked.

"I'd like to think it's because we both dove and pushed her out of the way."

"I'd like to think that too but it's probably not the reason."

"Then what was it?" Dan asked.

"I've been thinkin' that the bullet wasn't meant for Debbie at all. It was meant for you."

Chapter 41

Pam flopped down on the couch.
It wasn't fair
It just wasn't fair.
She had it all. Money, freedom, fun, secrets. But it lasted for such a short time. One simple call had turned her world upside-down.
And it wasn't just that. Sure, she wanted to continue with the life style she had been enjoying lately. That's what she really wanted.
But to do so meant putting Debbie in danger. She might even be killed.
Dan for sure would die.
At least it would be fast and painless, she'd been promised. He would be given the choice to trade his life for Debbie's.
Pam knew without a doubt that Dan would trade his life for Debbie's.
The unexpected bolt of jealousy that shot through Pam startled her. No one had ever loved *her* like that.
But Dan loved Debbie with a passion that was too obvious to deny.
And that wasn't all. Debbie had it all.
She had a beautiful voice.
A great figure.
A gorgeous face.
And money. She had lots of money.
And fame.
Yes, she was the one who had it all.
It wasn't fair.

If Pam warned her about what was about to happen, Pam would lose the little she had. She might even turn up dead.

It was Pam or Debbie.

It was that simple, black and white. Pam felt she had no choice but to choose herself. But could she really do that? Would she be able to live with herself?

Pam felt a sharp pain in the pit of her stomach. She swallowed hard and ignored it. She would survive. She would continue to enjoy the finer things in life as she had been destined to do.

Once she had decided that this was the route she was going to take, she reached for the phone and began to dial.

Chapter 42

It was tough being a woman in a man's domain, but that had never stopped Loyce Guthrie. She had been on the Dallas police force less than a year, but had already been commended several times for her outstanding work. One day she would be a renowned cop—maybe even as well respected as Harry Bronson. That was her dream, and she spent every second of her life pursuing that goal.

Except for right now.

Today, all she wanted to do was laze around until it was time to go to work. She planned to enjoy her morning off by taking a nice, long, relaxing bath. She went to the bathroom and turned on the hot water faucet.

The phone rang.

Let it ring. She was off duty.

The answering machine clicked on. "You'll hear a beep. You know what to do. I'll get back to you ASAP."

"Hi, Loyce, ma'am, this is Bronson. I'm here in Las Vegas, and I need your help. Seems—"

Loyce dove for the telephone. "Bronson, I'm here. What can I do for you?"

Bronson explained his urgency to find Derek Watson. "So I was thinkin' maybe I could fax you his picture and you could, uh, check around. See if we have anythin' on him. Now, if you're busy, I understand that. This is strictly a favor, and you don't have to do it."

"Except that I want to."

Silence. Then, "You do?"

"Yep."

"You don't have to."

"I know. I want to."

"That's great news. I'll fax the picture over to the department."

"I'm on my way." And why not? After all, she didn't have to be at work until three today. That gave her several hours to dig and search. "I'll get back to you as soon as possible."

She hung up, grabbed her wallet and keys, and headed toward the Dallas police station. She turned on the radio and sang aloud. This particular tune wasn't one of her favorite songs, but she still sang. She felt so happy. After all, it wasn't every day she got to do a favor for Harry Bronson.

Five minutes later she was back inside her apartment. She turned off the hot water.

Chapter 43

For once, rehearsal went exceptionally well. Bill looked pleased, and Debbie hoped he wasn't going to yell at her for being late.

No such luck.

Bill looked at all the dancers and performers. "Great job. Let's do it like this in tonight's performance. You're free to go. Debbie, you stay."

Once the stage was empty, Bill turned to Debbie. "What in the hell is going on? You were an hour late."

"I know. I'm sorry. It won't happen again."

"That's not good enough. I want an explanation."

Debbie sighed. "You're going to hear about this anyway. I guess you might as well hear it from me." She took a deep breath. "Someone shot at me today."

"What?"

"I said someone—"

"I know what you said." He raked his hair with his fingers. "Do you have any idea what this can do to the show?"

"I'm fine. Thank you for asking."

Bill looked at her and then down. "I'm sorry. I should have asked if you're okay. Are you?"

"Yes."

Bill nodded. "Good. Is the shooting related to . . . to . . . uh, what happened before?"

Debbie knew Bill would assume this shooting had been related to her prior experience when she first joined the show. "None at all. The police are saying it was a drive-by, and the shooter wasn't really aiming at me. He was just firing at random."

"And you happened to be there."

"What can I say? I'm such a lucky girl."

"Not so lucky. You are by far the best Colette impersonator I've ever seen, but impersonators in this city are a dime a dozen. You can and will be replaced if you tarnish Colette's image."

"I know that."

"Then you also know that I will have to report this."

What she knew was that this incident would generate publicity and any publicity was always good. Yet Bill claimed otherwise even though he knew better. What he really feared was that Colette's image would be tarnished, and Bill, who had desperately loved Colette, would do anything to keep that from happening. Debbie nodded and walked away. Anthony and Sylvia followed close behind.

By the time Debbie reached her suite, she felt drained. She wished Anthony and Sylvia would go away. She wanted to be alone, but she knew they would never leave her. "I guess I'm a bit more shook up about what happened than I thought I was. If it's okay with both of you, I'm going to take a nap."

Sylvia put her arm around Debbie. "You've got every right to be shook up. You go ahead and rest. Anthony and I will watch some TV and keep the volume very low."

Debbie nodded. "Thanks."

The phone rang.

Debbie glared at it, then picked it up.

"Debbie, I'm glad you're there. I didn't know if you'd be because I don't have your schedule. Oh by the way, just in case you don't recognize me, it's me, Pam. I hope I'm not bothering you."

"No, of course not." She looked at her watch. "My appointment with you isn't for two more hours, right? Or did I mess up, and I'm late?"

"No, silly, we're on for two hours from now, but I need to talk to you."

Debbie looked longingly toward the bedroom. Just a fifteen-minute nap. That's all she wanted. Fifteen minutes. "How about if we meet in an hour?"

"No, can't wait. This has to be taken care of right away."

"What is it?"

"Not over the phone. I'm home. I need for you to come to my house. There's something I have to show you. I know this is exactly what Dan is looking for."

Debbie's senses woke up. If she were a soldier, she'd be standing at attention. "I'll be there, but I have some friends visiting me from Hollywood. I'd have to bring them along."

"No problem. If you trust them with Dan's quest, then I trust them too."

Debbie wrote down the address and directions to her house. She hung up and turned to Sylvia. "Looks like no nap for me. That was Pam. She says she has something to show me and wants me—us—to go over right away."

Sylvia and Anthony exchanged looks. "What are the possibilities of this being a trap?" Sylvia asked.

The question gave Debbie pause. "I hadn't though of that. I don't see why it should be a trap. Pam wouldn't. . .Pam isn't. . ." She shrugged.

Sylvia retrieved her cell phone. "Just in case, I'm calling it in." She punched in Bronson's number instead of the police station's number.

Debbie looked away and wondered what Pam was up to.

Chapter 44

Bronson sat at the desk facing Dan and watched him work, or rather, not work.

Dan stared out the window. He opened and closed his drawer several times. He turned on the computer. He turned it off.

"Thought you were supposed to be workin'."

"I can't seem to concentrate. All I keep thinking is that this day is almost over, and I'm no further ahead in finding my daughter or even knowing if she's alive. I've done nothing about exposing Prickett, and Barbara Bloomer is about to come down on me like a Scud missile."

"Worst comes to worst, we get the police involved. In the meantime, I'd say Debbie's in pretty good hands."

"I'm sure she is, but—"

Bronson's cell phone rang and four people in the office including Dan, looked at their phones. Bronson felt like saying, "It's mine. I win," but refrained himself.

"Bronson here."

"This is Loyce Guthrie. I got what you wanted."

Bronson looked at his watch. It had only been a bit over three hours since he called and faxed her the picture. This lady was definitely destined to be on the top. "What have you got?"

"Derek was arrested once for drinking and driving which was good. That got him in the system but Derek Watson isn't his real name. It's Randall Dizon."

"If Derek is an alias, how did you find him?"

"The picture you sent, I used it to get a computer match. It literally gave me thousands of possibilities. I narrowed it down to Las Vegas. That cut it to several hundred.

I did a visual and I'm sure he's one of a half-a-dozen, and if I'm right, I'm betting on Randall Dizon."

"If that's your guess, I'll go with him too."

"I'm ready to fax you the pictures and information on each of these six people. Do I fax them to the same number you used to send me the picture?"

"That'll work."

"Good. Are you ready to receive?"

Bronson covered the mouthpiece. "Can we receive some faxes?"

Dan nodded.

Bronson removed his hand from the mouthpiece. "Go ahead and send them." He got up and headed toward the fax machine. "Loyce, you did good. Thanks for your help."

"My pleasure. Any time you need me—"

"I'll call you," Bronson hung up and then waited to retrieve the papers from the fax machine. When they arrived, he handed Dan the pictures.

He studied each. When he got to the fourth one, Dan pointed to it. "That's him. We got him!"

"Let's take a look."

Dan handed Bronson the picture. Bronson looked at the name, and noticed it was the same one Loyce Guthrie had predicted it would be. "Lookee here, says he's an actor."

"Does the paperwork give an address?"

Bronson scanned the information. "Yep, right here."

"Let's go pay him a visit."

They had almost reached Dan's car when Bronson's phone rang once again.

"Uncle Harry."

Bronson stopped when he recognized Sylvia's voice. "Everythin' okay?"

"Yes, I'm just calling to let you know that Pam called. She wants to show Debbie something that she claims is urgent. We're on our way to Pam's house now."

"What's the address?"

Sylvia gave it to him and Bronson copied it down. "Do you want us to join you?"

"I don't think that will be necessary. We'll check the place first and make sure all is okay, but we don't expect any problems."

"In that case, me and Dan, we'll be headin' to check on Derek Watson. We're followin' a lead that says he's an actor named Randall Dizon."

"Be careful."

"Sure enough. You, too."

They reached the car and climbed in.

"Maybe I'll finally get to see Diana." Dan bit his lip and started the car.

Chapter 45

Pam felt as nervous as a lamb in a slaughterhouse. Debbie and her friends should be here within the hour. That meant that they—whoever *they* were—should be arriving any minute now.

Maybe it wasn't too late to back out. She could grab the car keys and start driving and never look back. But no, that wouldn't work. They would find her. They were professionals.

Pam stared at the car keys. Her hand froze on top of them.

The doorbell rang and Pam jumped.

Too late, too late, too late.

It was beginning.

She opened the door and four husky-looking men entered. They didn't bother to introduce themselves. One man, wearing a gray polo shirt with the words Sedona, Arizona, embroidered on the shirt pocket, nodded at her. "Let's check the place, and let's be quick about it," he said as he brushed past Pam.

Pam watched as he paced in the entryway. The other three men went into the living room. Pam plastered herself against the wall and silently watched the men.

Sedona opened the coat closet in the vestibule, stuck his head in, then stepped inside, closing the door behind him. Seconds later he stepped out. "That will do."

Two others, one in a blue dress shirt and the other in a black T-shirt, busied themselves moving a large bookcase from the living room into the entryway. They placed it next to the door, positioning it in such a way as to leave enough space behind it so that one of the men could hide there.

The leader nodded and smiled. "All's set, then. All we've got to do is wait for Debbie to arrive."

Pam took a step forward. "What about me? What do I do?"

Sedona looked at her as though seeing her for the first time. "Main thing we want from you is to open the door as if nothing is going to happen. Make sure they come all the way in. If they get spooked out there, they're likely to take off running. We don't want that to happen. So you let them in, nice and easy. Once they're in, we'll take care of the two bodyguards, and my buddy here will take care of Debbie."

"What if the bodyguards want to come in and check out the place first?"

"Let them. We'll be hiding, remember? Once all three are in, that's when we'll grab them. Now, do you think you can handle that?"

Pam tried to say she could, but her voice failed her. She nodded.

"In the meantime, act natural. Do what you'd normally do."

Pam nodded and turned the television on. She sat on the couch, staring at the TV set. Her mind could not grasp what the actors were saying. Instead, she focused on each little noise generated outside her house.

A car sped by. A dog barked. Some kids squealed. Had her neighborhood always been this noisy?

Soon Debbie and her bodyguards would arrive. Debbie would be safe. They needed her alive, but her bodyguards, they might get killed. Would she be responsible for their deaths?

Pam leaned back into the couch. Her mouth felt so dry.

Dan will die, of that, she was sure.

A cold chill covered her body. She sat up and cleared her throat. Maybe after they kill Dan, they'll kill Debbie too.

That would make how many deaths? Four? She would be responsible for killing four people. Could she live with herself?

A small, animal-like noise escaped from her throat. She looked at the men to see if any of them had noticed. If they did, they didn't say anything. She stood up.

Sedona blocked her way. "And where do you think you're going?"

"I'm going to. . .water my plants." She pointed to the man to her right. "He told me to act normal, and at this time I always water my garden out front."

"You think we're that stupid? You've chickened out, haven't you? You'll be outside watering, and as soon as Debbie drives up, you're going to warn her. Is that the plan?"

Panic shot through Pam like a lightning bolt. Was she that easy to read? "No, of course not. If I had planned to warn Debbie, I would have done it a long time ago."

"Good answer. Don't even think about double crossing us or you'll end up dead. Now, sit down."

Pam sat and in her minds eye let out a scream, *Debbie, don't come. Please don't come.*

How could she warn Debbie? How could she not warn her? Oh God, what could she do?

Pam felt the blood drain from her face when she heard a car pull up her driveway.

"They're here." Blue shirt watched them from the small opening in the closed curtains.

"Let's get into position," Sedona said. He turned to Pam, "One false move, and you'll be the first to die."

Pam felt the blood drain from her face.

Each of the men went to their designated hiding areas.

The doorbell rang.

Chapter 46

"That's them. Those are the apartments." Bronson pointed to the two-story white stucco structure on the other side of the street from them.

Dan executed a left turn and slowly drove past each unit. The first set included numbers 100 through 160 and 200 through 260. Derek/Randall lived in Apartment 177. Dan drove to the second set of buildings and parked the car.

Bronson looked at him. "You ready?"

No, he would never be ready. "Do I have a choice?"

"We always have choices."

"How philosophical."

"I try."

They got out and rang the doorbell.

No one answered.

They rang again.

Still no answer.

"He's bound to come home sometime. I'm going to sit here until he arrives." Dan crossed his arms.

"And if he sees you sitting here, he's likely not to stop."

Dan frowned. "Must you always be so logical?"

"I try."

"So what does your logical mind suggest we do?"

"We check with the neighbors, see if any of 'em have seen a little girl."

Dan shrugged, not because he agreed, but because he couldn't think of what else to do. He followed Bronson to Apartment 178.

The door opened before Bronson had a chance to ring the doorbell. An elderly lady stared at them. Her small frame made her look fragile. In spite of the hot weather, she wore a thin, baby blue sweater that hung loosely from her shoulders. "I saw you coming out of Randall's apartment. Are you his friends?"

"Not really. Why?" Dan asked.

"He seemed awfully worried, last time I saw him." She smacked her lips. "Maybe I'm using the wrong word. It wasn't so much worried as frightened."

"Do you know, ma'am, why he was frightened?"

She bit her lip and stared first at Bronson then at Dan. "You best be going." She started to slam the door shut, but Bronson shoved his foot in, preventing her from doing so.

"We need to talk to you," Dan said.

The old woman's eyes widened. "I'll call the police."

Bronson flashed her a disarming smile. "My apologies if we scared you, ma'am, but we're the good guys. We're not going to hurt you or Randall."

"How do I know you're the good guys?"

Bronson showed her his badge. "You're right, ma'am, Randall is in a heap of trouble, and we want to help him. I'm sure you do too."

"How can I help?" She opened the door a bit more, but did not invite them in.

"You can answer some questions, and you can begin by giving us your name." Bronson retrieved his spiral notebook and pen from his shirt pocket.

"I'm Terra Ager. I've known Randall since he was a little boy. What kind of a trouble is he in?"

Bronson wrote down some information and looked up at her. He gave her his wide-eyed, innocent, puppy-dog look. "I'm afraid I'm not at liberty to answer that. What I can tell you is that anything you tell us will help Randall."

"What is it that you want to know?"

"Why do you think he was frightened?"

Terra shook her head. "I don't know. All he'd tell me was that the less I know, the better off I'd be."

"When was the last time you saw him?"

She squinted and thought for a moment. "Three, four days ago."

"That would make it around the same time when I last saw him," Dan said.

"Do you think something dreadful has happened to him?" She seemed on the verge of tears. "I'm so worried about him."

"Best not to worry, ma'am." Bronson reached out and patted her shoulder. "We'll look for him. What can you tell us about his wife and kid?"

She gasped. "Didn't you know? She left him. Packed up everything while he was away at work. He came home to an almost empty apartment. Broke my heart. His, too, I'm sure."

"What about. . .the child?" Dan asked.

"You mean Leslie?"

Dan nodded and tried not to swallow too hard. So Diana had been renamed Leslie. He hated the thought of her having a different name.

"She took the child with her, of course. Any mom worth anything always drags the kids along."

"What address did she give you, ma'am?"

Terra's eyebrows arched. "How did you know she gave me. . . I mean, how would I know that?"

"Like I told you, ma'am. Randall's in a heap of trouble, and if you want to help him, you'll give me that address."

"I don't see what one has to do with the other."

"Mighty good chance, ma'am, that Randall turned to his wife in time of need."

"Could be, but that doesn't mean I have the address."

"My mistake, ma'am. For a minute there, I thought you wanted to help Randall." Bronson closed his notebook, clicked his pen shut, and turned to Dan. "Come on, let's go."

The old lady grabbed Bronson's arm. "Wait. Maybe I do remember her giving me her new address. I suppose it won't hurt to give it to you."

"No, ma'am. It wouldn't hurt at all."

Chapter 47

Much to Dan's dismay, Bronson refused to leave until they checked Randall's apartment. "And how do you suppose we get in? Neither of us have a key." Dan drove around the block so that the old woman would think they had left.

Bronson smiled.

Dan looked at him. "You're planning to break-in into his apartment, aren't you?"

Bronson's smile widened.

"What kind of policeman are you anyway?"

"The unorthodox kind. The one who is close to retirement and doesn't always play it by the book."

"I gathered as much."

"That's what makes you an outstanding reporter."

Dan pulled into the apartment building's back parking lot. They used the late evening shadows to conceal their presence and made it all the way to Randall's door without attracting any attention.

"Now what?" Dan asked.

"Now we go in." Bronson turned the knob and went inside Randall's apartment.

"Man, you're fast." Dan followed him in and closed the door behind him.

"When you breaking into an apartment it's best not to dilly-dally."

"So, we won't be here long, then?" Dan reached for the light switch.

"Don't you dare."

"Why not?"

"Dead give-away. Neighbors will know someone's home. Let's do with the little light we have."

"What are we looking for, anyway?"

"A body."

Dan froze. "You serious?"

"I'm hopin' we don't find one, and I'm prayin' we'll find somethin' that will give us a clue."

"A clue to what?"

"Anythin'. Right now, I reckon I'm just lookin'."

Dan bit his tongue to keep from saying something rude. Instead of wasting time here, they should be heading to Mrs. Randall Dizon's house. Dan stayed in the entryway while Bronson walked around the five-room apartment.

It took Bronson less than five minutes not to find what he was looking for. He returned empty-handed.

"Satisfied?" Dan asked.

"Quite satisfied actually."

They stepped out, closed and locked the door behind them, and headed for the car.

"Mrs. Dizon must have been real angry," Bronson said.

"Why do you say that?"

"She took every single picture of the little girl with her."

"I guess that's only natural. She'd want to have her daughter's pictures."

"You know, you're probably right."

They got inside the car and Dan sped off.

"Funny thing," Bronson said.

"What's that?"

"I did find a picture of a little boy."

Dan looked at him.

"Do you suppose that might be Leslie?"

Chapter 48

"Slow down, slow down." Bronson held onto both sides of the car seat and tried to maintain his upright position. "Remember, you're ridin' with an officer of the law. I have been known to give out a ticket or two."

"You have no jurisdiction in Vegas. You said so yourself."

"Ever heard of a citizens' arrest?"

"Yep, but I've never heard of a citizens' ticket."

"There's always a first time for everythin'."

Dan stole a quick glance at the speedometer. The needle hovered between seventy-five and eighty. Bronson was right. He should slow down. "I just want to be sure we get there before Diana goes to sleep."

"We may not get there at all the way you're driving."

Dan slowed down.

Bronson looked out the window. "You shouldn't get your hopes up, you know."

Yes, he knew, but he couldn't help it. Dan exited I-15, turned right, and followed the streets to his destination.

The house turned out to be no more than a small cube in a modest neighborhood. Lights shined from two different windows. That meant that someone had to be home. A gray Ford truck was parked in the carport. Dan pulled in behind it.

Bronson rang the doorbell.

They waited.

Dan rang the doorbell. "Not again. Someone's got to be home." He formed a fist and pounded it against the door. The door opened about six inches.

"Now, you're in trouble," Bronson said. He pushed Dan out of the way, retrieved his gun from the small of his back, and plastered himself against the door.

"I didn't know you were armed."

"What kind of a detective would travel without a gun?" Bronson whispered. He put his index finger to his lips, telling him not to respond. Using his leg, he pushed the door open the rest of the way.

Dan stood perfectly still as he waited.

Bronson stuck his head in. He crouched and scanned the area from behind his gun. "Looks like nobody's here." He relaxed his stance, but kept the gun by his side. "But looks like somebody's been here."

Chairs were overturned. Papers and broken pieces of glass and other debris were scattered on the floor. Bronson raised the gun in a ready-to-shoot position. "Wait here." He went deeper into the house.

Dan stood in the entryway surveying the mess. Bronson was the expert, but it took no expert to recognize the signs of a struggle.

Bronson returned. He had put the gun away. "We should get to a phone," he said.

"To report a body?" Dan hesitated as he asked the question.

"Yep."

"Whose?"

"Randall's/Derek's."

"Dead?"

"As the potted plant in my office."

"And. . .and. . ."

"No trace of the child."

Dan closed his eyes and sighed. Another dead-end.

"I'll drive you to a phone."

"Don't bother. I've changed my mind."

"You plan on using this phone to call the police?" Dan pointed to the wall phone in Randall's/Derek's living room.

"Nope. Don't plan to call at all." Bronson walked out and Dan followed him. They headed for the car.

"Why not?"

"The police will know we've gotten this far."

They reached the car and got in. Dan started the engine and drove off. "I don't understand."

"Remember me tellin' you that the shootin' at the Meadows Mall parkin' lot didn't make much sense? That I thought that the bullet was meant for you and not Debbie?"

Dan nodded.

"That's why the shooter missed. In tryin' to protect Debbie, you moved just at the right moment."

"But why would he be aiming at me?"

"You're the one tryin' to find Diana."

"So you think Derek, uh, Randall, took a shot at me to keep me from finding Diana?"

"No, I don't think that at all. It's somethin' Anthony pointed out to me. You reported finding Lakeyshia's body. Soon after that, you get shot. Someone knew right away that you had been the one who called in the murder."

"But I didn't leave a name."

"Precisely. Yet, the police knew and the bad guys knew too. That means there's a leak somewhere. I'd bet a year's salary it's in the police department. Who's in charge of this case?"

"Ralph Simpson."

Bronson frowned.

"No, you're wrong. It can't be he. He's always been so. . .so. . ." Dan shook his head. "I just don't think it's Ralph."

"I don't know this man, but I do know of him, and what I do know is not necessarily good. Still, I'll reserve judgment until I know all of the details. All I'm sayin' is that we should check every angle out. You never know where that will lead."

Dan nodded.

Bronson adjusted his seat belt. "These are just theories, you understand? Maybe tomorrow, we can have another meetin' and toss all of our ideas on the table. Tonight, I want to think about them."

"I'll drop you off and see you tomorrow."

"I'd advise you to get a good night's rest. You'll need your strength for tomorrow."

Dan focused his attention on passing the driver in front of him. He was weaving a bit too much for Dan's taste. After a few failed attempts, Dan successfully passed him. "Good advice."

"But you're not going to take it."

"In a way, yes. All I plan to do is talk to Debbie. I'm anxious to hear what Pam had to say." Dan looked at the clock in the dashboard. "It's almost ten. I can catch the last few minutes of her show. Then she'll be free for about an hour or so."

"Sounds like a plan."

"Not much of one." Dan pulled over at the casino's main entrance and let Bronson out. He then found a parking spot and headed for the entrance closest to the show.

As usual, the casino thrived with noise and a hint of excitement. Dan walked past the rows of slot machines and headed toward the back of the room where the theater was located.

Dan reached for the VIP door and felt someone stop him.

"I wouldn't go in there if I were you."

Dan turned. He recognized Julio, one of the waiters who served the audience their drinks while the show was going on. "Why shouldn't I go in?"

"You don't know?"

Dan shook his head.

"Debbie didn't show up, and she didn't even bother to call."

Dan took off at a gallop.

Chapter 49

As soon as Pam opened the door, Debbie knew by the look on Pam's face that something was wrong. Her suspicions were reaffirmed when Pam mouthed the word *go*. Debbie took a step backward and said, "Hi, Pam. I'll see you in a second. I forgot my purse in the car."

"Car's locked. I'll go open it for you." As Sylvia spoke, she tried to place herself between Pam and Debbie, but before she could successfully do it, a shot rang out.

Pam collapsed. Debbie drew in her breath and caught her.

She looked up and two men stood at the door, both pointing a gun at her.

Sedona cocked the gun but looked at Anthony and Sylvia. "If you don't want anything to happen to Debbie's beautiful face, I'd advise you to come in very peaceful like. No sudden moves."

Sylvia moved toward Debbie. "Let me help you with Pam." When she was mostly hidden behind Debbie, she quickly retrieved the small handgun that she kept strapped to her right hip. She placed it under Pam's belt at the small of her back. "Is she still alive?"

"I. . .I think so. She's breathing, but barely." Debbie felt like screaming but she forced herself to follow Sylvia's lead. She recognized the importance of remaining calm.

"Get inside!" Sedona ordered.

Sylvia and Debbie carried Pam in and laid her on the couch. "She needs immediate medical attention," Sylvia said.

"That's too bad," the black shirt answered, "'cuz none of us are doctors."

That produced a chuckle from two of the armed men, but not from Sedona. He grabbed Debbie's hair and yanked it down. Debbie let out a startled yelp. He placed the gun at her forehead.

Debbie felt her legs turn to jell-o. Only sheer will kept her standing up. She bit her lip to keep from screaming.

Sedona looked at Anthony, then at Sylvia. "Debbie told Pam that you two are visiting from California, is that so?"

Sylvia nodded. "Hollywood, to be precise."

"Hollywood." He made a face to show he wasn't impressed. "Funny, I wouldn't have placed either of you from Hollywood. You look more like locals. Do you know what I mean, Officer Ulan and Officer Sanchez?"

Debbie felt the blood drain from her face, but she noticed that neither Sylvia's nor Anthony's features revealed anything.

"Let's have those weapons, nice and easy, or this lady gets it."

Both Anthony and Sylvia took out their 9mm Barrettas and set them by their feet.

"Kick them this way."

They did.

Brown shirt picked them up and pocketed them. Blue shirt frisked them for any concealed weapons. He didn't find any.

Sedona released Debbie. She almost tumbled to the ground, but caught herself.

Sedona kept his gun pointed out, but no longer aimed it at anyone. "Now we're going to wait. Dan knows you came here. When he notices you're gone, he'll go looking for you, and this is the first place he's going to come. So let's all sit and wait."

Sylvia sat down on the couch by Pam's feet. Both Anthony and Debbie sat on the smaller couch.

"Uh, uh. You sit on the floor." He pointed at Anthony. "And you. Go sit over there by yourself." He pointed to the opposite side of the room.

Once they were seated, Sedona continued, "Let's hand over the phones. We don't want you accidentally making a call or sending some kind of message."

He collected them and smiled.

All they had to do now was wait for Dan to show up.

The trap was set.

Chapter 50

Bronson felt lousy. Here it was almost ten and his poor Carol had been alone all day. Not much of a vacation for her. Maybe when this Dan ordeal was finished, he could take a couple of extra days. After all, he had more than enough vacation time coming.

He carefully opened the door to his motel room. Carol would probably be asleep now, or she'd be curled up in bed wearing her little blue cotton nightgown and watching a TV movie.

Instead, she was fully dressed in an elegant, yet simple, summer dress. "There you are." She reached for her purse.

Bronson stood by the door, not sure how to react.

Carol looked at her watch. "You've got exactly three minutes to freshen up. Then, we're going out."

"Going out?"

"Yes. Haven't you heard? This is Las Vegas, the city that never closes."

"Where are we going?"

"I thought we'd begin by taking a nice leisurely stroll down The Strip. Then maybe we can do some casino hopping. We don't have to gamble, but I surely want to visit some of these casinos." She looked at her watch once again. "You've wasted a whole minute now. You only have two left before we walk out."

Bronson made a mad dash to the bathroom.

Four minutes later, he was ready. He noticed Carol never mentioned the extra two minutes.

He was about to close the door behind them when Carol stopped. Imitating her husband, she hit her forehead with the palm of her hand. "Oh, silly me. I almost forgot."

"What's that?"

"Your cell phone, my dear."

Bronson looked at her, a question mark stamped on his face.

"Hand me your cell phone."

He did.

She walked back into the room, set the phone down in the middle of the bed, and walked back out. "Tonight, you're all mine."

She kissed his lips.

They were getting in the elevator when the cell phone rang.

The voice mail picked up.

Chapter 51

Dan unlocked the door to Debbie's suite and threw it open. "Debbie!" His voice caught in his throat.

He checked the bedroom, the bathroom, the kitchen, and the living room. He stepped out onto the balcony. He even checked behind the wet bar, inside the shower, and inside the closet. She was nowhere.

He punched in Debbie's cell number, but got only her pre-recorded message. "Debbie, wherever you are, I'll be there. I'm coming for you, babe. Just be safe." He hung up and called Sylvia. On the sixth ring, another voice mail answered.

Dan did not leave a message.

Next, he called Bronson.

Another machine.

"Debbie's missing. She doesn't answer her phone. Neither does Sylvia. It's 9:57. I'm going to Pam's."

He considered calling Pam's house, but if she was responsible for Debbie's disappearance, he didn't want to alert her.

He ran out of the suite.

* * *

"Now there's a sweet message if I've ever heard one." Sedona held the cell phone out toward Debbie. "You want to hear it? It's from Dan. He tells you to be safe and he's coming for you." He threw his head back and laughed.

"What if he calls the police?" A frown creased the blue shirt's forehead and he wrung his hands.

Sedona shrugged. "So? Ralph Simpson will take care of that. Why do you suppose we've been paying him for all of these years?"

Sylvia looked down and inwardly frowned. So Anthony had been right. Ralph Simpson was on their payroll. That clarified a lot of things, and it also answered her biggest question: what were they going to do with them once Dan showed up.

The answer was crystal clear. They were going to kill them. These goons didn't care what they said and that was because in their mind, they were already dead.

She looked at Anthony who sat on the floor across the room from her. She rested her chin on her hand. In so doing, she extended her index finger and stuck her thumb out, forming the shape of a gun.

Anthony reached down and scratched his ankle.

Good. He still had his concealed weapon strapped to his ankle. The twerps who had frisked them hadn't even noticed it.

She too had her weapon. Sort of. It was in the small of Pam's back. That wasn't a very good place for it. In case of an emergency, it'd be hard to reach.

If only she could get to it.

Pam moaned and Sylvia, who sat on the floor next to the couch, looked at her. "She's shivering. There's a blanket on top of the couch. Would you mind if I cover her?"

"Makes no difference to me."

Sylvia looked at Anthony, then at Pam's waist and back up at Anthony.

Anthony's nod was barely perceptible.

Sylvia reached for the blanket and tucked it around Pam. Most of the blanket dragged on the floor.

Anthony stood up. "I need to use the bathroom. Any of you gentlemen care to come with me?"

They looked from one to another.

"You—" Sedona pointed to black shirt. "Go with him."

While they were busy talking, Sylvia grasped the opportunity to retrieve the gun from Pam's belt. Using the blanket as a cover, she slid the gun down and under the couch. Now it was within easy reach.

All she needed was the opportunity to use it.

Chapter 52

Like an unending river, hundreds of ideas, questions, and scenarios flowed through Dan's mind as he sped toward Pam's house. What could he do?

What should he do?

"Think like a policeman," Sylvia had said.

What would a policeman do? He'd call for back up. Bronson was unavailable. Sylvia and Anthony were who-knows-where. That left the police.

Should he call the police? Anthony had told Bronson that he suspected Ralph Simpson of being a crooked cop. If he called the police would that somehow complicate matters? He couldn't see how. After all, only one cop was on the take, not the entire police force.

Traffic on I-15 came to an abrupt stop. There must have been an accident up ahead or construction, or both. Dan slammed his hands on the steering wheel. Why now? His exit was only two or three miles ahead.

He grabbed his cell phone and dialed 9. . .1. . . He hesitated. His lane moved. He advanced ten car lengths. He cleared the phone. He was able to move some more.

Once he reached Pam's house, he'd be able to evaluate the situation. Then he'd call the police.

He moved some more again. This time only three car lengths, if that much.

Dan cursed himself for taking the freeway. He knew better.

* * *

Bronson had to admit this was nice. Strolling The Strip with his beautiful wife by his side, stopping wherever they wanted to, for as long as they wanted to. Good thing about The

Strip, it was as bright as it could be. Bronson had heard that The Strip contained so many lights that anyone walking down The Strip could read a book in the middle of the night. He had doubted it. Now he knew it was true.

And the weather was perfect too. Not hot like during the day. Just nice. Now and then a cool breeze blew and that made it that much nicer.

Bronson reached for Carol's hand.

Two lovers in Las Vegas. No cares in the world. Just enjoying the lights, the sounds, the sights. Ah, this was life at its best.

Up ahead, the Crystal Palace Casino's white marble statues of royalty in chariots drawn by elegant horses beckoned them. They stood and admired the superbly done statues of horsemen and parading troops looking out toward a rainbow of flowers.

Inside the casino, Bronson knew, Dan and Debbie would be enjoying a nice, warm cup of coffee, talking about what Pam had told her. He wished he were part of their conversation. Anthony and Sylvia would be there too.

His Carol would enjoy seeing her niece again. And Anthony too. Why she could finally meet Debbie. Bronson turned to Carol. "How about if we go inside the casino?"

Carol stopped. "Can't you take a few hours off, Harry Bronson? My God, it's our vacation."

Gee, that woman sure could read him. Sometimes, it was just plain exasperating. "No, this isn't work—a social call. I thought maybe you'd like to meet Debbie and visit with Anthony and Sylvia."

Carol shook her head. "Okay, whatever."

Chapter 53

Dan could see his exit sign. All he needed was to move forward a few car lengths. Then he'd be free to maneuver away from traffic and toward his exit.

"Come on. Move. Move. Move!"

As though the traffic jam had heard him, his lane began to roll. Minutes later, Dan took the off ramp and headed toward Pam's house.

Think like a policeman.

He approached Pam's street at a normal speed. Just one of the guys in the neighborhood, heading home. He studied the area. Dan estimated the houses sold in the mid-fifties to mid-sixties range. He read the street numbers. According to his estimates, Pam's house should be located on the next block, third one down to his left.

He pulled off, parked, and spotted Pam's house. He could see Debbie's car parked in the driveway.

Think like a policeman.

He called Bronson. Again, the voice mail kicked in. "I can see Pam's house from where I stand. Debbie's car is in the driveway. There aren't any bushes, and the windows on the front and side of the house are large, so if they're looking out, they might be able to see me. I did notice that the curtains are closed so maybe I might be able to sneak in. Once I get there, I'm not sure what I'll do. I hope I don't blow it. If anything happens to Debbie, or Sylvia, or Anthony. . ." He paused and tried to think of what else he should say. He couldn't come up with anything, so he added, "Just wish me luck."

He closed the phone and stared at it. Against his better judgment, he called the police and explained why he thought that Debbie, Sylvia, and Anthony might be held prisoners at

Pam's house. He gave them the address and hung up.

This time before closing the phone, he set it on the vibrate mode. He got out of the car and crossed the street so that Pam's house would now be to his right. He kept as close to the houses as possible, hoping he couldn't be seen even if someone inside Pam's house was looking out the window.

His heart pounded hard as he turned and headed up the side of Pam's house.

At the first window, the curtains were drawn, but at the one further back, they remained open. Dan bent down as he went past the first window and maintained the crouching position until he reached the window with an open curtain.

He glanced in and saw a bedroom. His quick eye caught a couple of details. A dresser drawer wide open. An unmade bed. A lamp on top of the dresser with its bulb burning. Nothing there would help him. He moved on.

Around the corner was the backyard. He peeked around the edge of the house and whispered a small thank you. Someone had turned on the porch light on and Dan could see that the yard was empty and that all the window shades facing the backyard were opened.

He looked in the first window. Same bedroom, different view. The next window was higher up and had thicker, opaque glass. Probably the bathroom. Dan moved on.

The living room. One quick glance told him all he had to know. Debbie, Sylvia, and Anthony were alive, all sitting on the floor on opposite sides of the room. Dan had not been able to see any sign of Pam, unless she was the figure resting on the couch.

Dan also noticed that four tough looking men were with them. They seemed to be impatient.

Dan considered his options. Best thing was to update Bronson, but not from here. Dan didn't want to take the chance that one of the men would hear him talking.

As quickly as possible, he returned to the front yard.

The dog next door began to bark. Dan felt his heart beat accelerate. Would the noise cause Debbie's captors to look out the window? Would they see him? He increased his speed and soon reached the corner's safety.

Feeling as though he had reached sanctuary, he called Bronson and left another message. "If I'm lucky, I might be able to attract Anthony's attention. He's sitting down, facing the backyard. If he can somehow get one of the men to go outside with him, we could overtake him. Then the two of us can go back and. . ." He paused, thinking about how it could go. "Anyway, that's my plan. Wish me luck."

He closed the phone and headed for Pam's backyard.

Chapter 54

"I don't like this," Sedona said. "Springer should have been here by now. What's taking him so long?"

No one answered.

He paced in the small area of Pam's living room. He walked over to where Anthony sat and kicked his left leg.

Anthony groaned.

Sedona took out his gun and pointed it at Anthony. "You, get up. Nice and easy. Any sudden moves and you're dead."

Anthony rubbed his leg and stood.

"This cramped place is getting to me. I can't think. I need fresh air. We're going to the backyard. I'll have my gun pointed at this officer all of the time. Anything happens here, he's dead." He stressed the word *officer* to show what a distaste that produced in his mouth.

They stepped out into the porch and closed the door.

"Did you have to kick me so hard?" Anthony rubbed his leg.

"Got to make it look good, don't we?"

"Bastard."

Sedona's eyes pierced Anthony's. "Just because you're a cop, that doesn't make you any better than me. We're both from the same pod. So if I were you, I'd watch that mouth. I could blow your brains out before you could reach the gun strapped to your ankle."

Anthony looked away. Mike Patterson, the man wearing the Sedona shirt, was definitely not one of his favorite people. "Speaking of guns, did you know Sylvia's got a gun under the couch?"

Patterson turned to look at Anthony. "I knew she had one, but I couldn't for the life of me figure out where. That's why we frisked you both. How'd she get it under the couch?"

"She outsmarted you. That's how."

"Since you're so wise, tell me how we can take the gun away from her without blowing your cover."

"Simple. Just have me sit where she is. I'll take care of the gun."

"Okay." He nodded. "Reason I got you out here is that I want to hear about Springer."

"What about him?"

"Why hasn't he shown up? You think he's up to something?"

"I don't know him that well, so I can't be sure, but if you ask me to take an educated guess, I'd say probably. He's intelligent and calculating. That always makes a dangerous combination."

"Using your educated guess, what do you think he'll do?"

"He'll probably call the police."

"Even though we made sure he knew Ralph Simpson is on the take?"

"That won't stop him."

"So what do you suggest we do?"

Anthony shrugged. "There's not much we can do, but sit and wait. If the police come by themselves, I'll be able to take care of them. If Dan's with them, then we'll have to take them prisoners too."

"Then what do we do with them?"

"Same as the rest. Kill them all."

Chapter 55

When Anthony and Patterson returned to the living room, Anthony looked at Pam. She lay on her side, her eyes closed, her face the shade of a vanilla shake. "How's she doing?"

Sylvia shook her head and looked down.

"Before I became a cop, I had a couple of pre-med classes. Mind if I look at her?"

Patterson shrugged. "She's a goner anyway. What do I care?" He pointed his gun at Sylvia. "You, up. Move to the other side of the room."

Sylvia stood up and went to the other side of the room.

"You can look at her now."

Anthony bent over her. He felt her forehead and searched for a pulse. He looked at the bullet hole in her upper back, close to the shoulder blade. "We've got to get her to a hospital."

Patterson laughed. "Great diagnosis, doctor. You would have made a great physician."

Anthony sat down on the floor in front of the couch, exactly where the gun would be. He put his hands behind his back.

* * *

Just as Anthony and Sedona stepped inside the living room, Dan turned toward Pam's backyard. His mind was so intent on catching Anthony's attention that Dan almost walked into the backyard without first checking it out.

He caught himself just in time. He paused at the corner of the house. No sound emanated from the yard. Dan stuck his head out and peeked. No one. He breathed easier. He could implement his plan, provided Anthony was still sitting in the same place.

He wasn't.

Frustration ate at Dan. He'd be dammed if he'd give up now.

Dan considered his alternatives. In order to capture Anthony's attention, Dan would have to do it from the window on the other side of the door. Going around the front of the house and into the yard from the other side would not work. When he had scouted the area, he had noticed that due to a high fence, the trash cans, and debris scattered on the right-hand side of the house, it was impossible to access the yard from that side.

That meant that if he were going to reach the other window, he would have to get past the open door. He cursed the porch light that illuminated the yard, the same one he had previously been thankful for. He drew in a big breath, carefully looked in the window above him, noticed that no one seemed to be interested in the backyard, grasped the opportunity, and dashed past the door.

One of the gunmen must have noticed something as he walked toward the door and looked at the yard. Had he stepped outside, he would have seen Dan. There was no place to hide.

Dan felt his heart pounding as he looked at the corner of the house. A six-foot fence and no gate prevented him from leaving the yard. The only way out was the way he had come.

Better make the best of circumstances. He peeked in the window, but Anthony wasn't looking his way.

One of the gunmen was talking and waving his gun at him. Anthony stood up and both headed toward the front of the house.

This was exactly what Dan wanted. Once outside, both he and Anthony would overtake the guard. Then they could work on the others.

But first he had to reach the front of the house, which meant retracing his steps and going past the open door.

But he couldn't.

That one gunman still stood guard by the backdoor. Dan would have to wait until he moved away from there.

The gunman reached out and opened the back door. Dan held his breath.

Chapter 56

Because of the street light brightly shining one house away, Blue Shirt had decided against turning on Pam's front porch light. This way, the house wasn't as well lit and drew little attention to itself. Yet, there was plenty of light to see what, if anything, was going on outside the front of the house.

Blue Shirt stood by the window and periodically split the curtains only enough to peek outside. So far so good. Then he stiffened. "We've got company," he said as a patrol car pulled to the curb across the street.

Brown Shirt who was about to step out into the backyard, closed the door, turned his attention to what was going on out front, but held on to the door handle.

Patterson looked out the window. He pointed his gun at Anthony. "You, come with me."

They stood on the porch, watching the policemen settle their gear on their hips and slowly cross the street.

"Hey, Billy. Joe." Anthony's smile reached all the way to his eyes. "What are you guys doing out here?"

The patrolmen stopped.

Anthony's smile widened as he approached them.

"We got a call. Possible kidnaping," the officer on the left said.

Anthony laughed. "Here? You mean here? Nah, me and my buddy. . ." He pointed to Patterson. ". . .we're just kicking back with three other guys."

"But all is okay?"

Anthony scratched his chin and pretended to be thinking. "One of the ladies got drunk and passed out on the couch. That leaves two ladies for the five of us. I don't know if you'd say that's okay."

The policemen laughed.

"Hey, why don't you guys come in? Have a drink with us."

One of the policemen shook his head. "Nah, better not. We're on duty."

"I'm not." Anthony wiggled his eyebrows.

The policemen smiled and turned when they heard a car door slam behind them. Their supervisor, Sgt. Chris Couch headed toward them.

"Hi, Sarge," the tallest of the two policemen said. "It's a false alarm. My partner, Billy, and I were just heading out."

"Yep," the other policeman said. "And before you ask, yes, Joe and I will do the paperwork when we get back to the station."

"In that case, there's no need for me to hang around here. I'll see you all later." With that, Chris left.

"Reckon we'll be going too," one policeman said to the other. "Anthony, you take care of yourself."

"Of course. Always."

Patterson and Anthony stood outside watching the departing police car.

Patterson turned to Anthony. "Are you crazy? Why did you invite them in?"

"I know how a cop's mind works. If I hadn't asked them in, they would have been suspicious. So I invite them in. They refuse. I don't invite them, they want to come in. Now relax. They're gone."

They headed back inside.

"See how easy that was?" Patterson looked at Blue Shirt. "We got rid of them just like that." He snapped his fingers.

"That was Billy and Joe," Anthony told Sylvia just as soon as he stepped back in.

Sylvia looked up at Anthony. "I like them."

"Shut up, both of you!" Patterson shoved Anthony. "Now go sit down like a good little cop."

* * *

As soon as the guard moved away from the backdoor, Dan grabbed the opportunity to head past the door and out toward the front of the house. He reached the front corner just in time to catch the tail end of Anthony's and the other man's conversation.

Dan stood, dumbfounded, trying to make sense of what he just heard.

Of course. It all made sense. Every stone Dan had turned led to a dead end, as if they knew what he was planning, what he was thinking.

All of this time, he had trusted Debbie to Anthony.

And Anthony was one of them.

Chapter 57

Dan headed away from Pam's house. This time, he didn't wait to reach the end of the block before he punched in Bronson's number.

Much to Dan's relief, this time Bronson picked up. "Dan, glad you called. I got your other messages. I'm on my way. I got a plan I've been—"

"Anthony is one of them."

A pause. Then, "You're sure?"

"Yes."

"Damn."

Dan briefly filled him in. "They're all back in the house, waiting for me to show up."

"Then you're going to go over there, ring the doorbell, and announce yourself. And while you're doing that, I'll come in the back."

"Then what?"

"Then we fight it out."

"That's it?"

"Yep."

"Doesn't seem like much of a plan to me."

"Nope."

"That's five against us two."

"There's Sylvia. Don't forget Sylvia."

"Okay. Three against five."

"And Debbie makes four."

"Shit, Bronson, Deb and I aren't trained professionals. There's only you and Sylvia."

"Maybe not." Bronson began to detail the rest of his plan.

Dan listened.

* * *

Dan had to wait seven minutes, but he was ready to go. He sat in the car, his fingers tapping the steering wheel.

When he saw Bronson, he sat up straight and waited some more. He looked at his watch and anxiously watched the seconds crawl by.

Bronson gave him the signal.

Dan started the engine and drove up to Pam's house. He pulled in the driveway, right next to Debbie's car. He got out and rang the doorbell.

One of the men Dan had seen answered the door.

Dan smiled. "You must be Pam's boyfriend. I'm Dan Springer. Listen, I'm having trouble with my car. Can you come out here and help me?"

"Sorry, I don't know anything about cars."

"No problem. You can hold the flashlight while I look at the engine." Dan turned toward his car.

"No, wait."

Dan continued to head toward the car. He heard the screen door close and footsteps following him. He hadn't reached the car when he felt a gun press against his spine.

"This isn't a good time to work on car problems, real or imaginary. Now, let's go inside."

* * *

With his gun drawn, Bronson entered the living room using the back door.

One man stood by the window, watching the events unfold out front. The other two stood guard over Debbie and Sylvia.

As soon as Sylvia saw Bronson, she reached under the couch, searching for the gun she knew she had placed there.

Brown Shirt raised his gun.

By now, Anthony had retrieved the gun strapped to his ankle. He aimed and fired.

Chapter 58

As soon as Dan and the man turned back toward the house, the police officers who had been hiding behind the parked cars in the driveway came out and surrounded Dan and the armed man.

He dropped the gun and raised his arms.

Inside the house, a shot rang out. Followed by another.

Three of the four policemen who were out front ran inside the house.

Two more policemen burst in through the back door.

Anthony was behind a big chair and Brown Shirt was shooting at him from the hallway. They had exchanged several shots when the police burst in suddenly. Brown Shirt jumped back giving Anthony an opening which he didn't waste. The bullet got Brown Shirt in the chest. He fell with a groan and a thud.

Bronson and Blue Shirt were exchanging rounds from the kitchen and the dining room. Bronson ducked down behind the counter. He popped up, took a shot, and was pelted with broken glass from a water pitcher Blue Shirt had managed to hit. Blood dripped down Bronson's cheek. He wiped his face and stared at the blood. His heart rate went to the roof. The sound of footsteps coming at him drenched him in fear. Was this the day his luck would run out?

He took a breath and crawled into the laundry room. Blue Shirt assaulted the kitchen with guns ablaze shooting at the spot Bronson had just vacated. When the flurry of shots ended, Bronson burst out from the laundry room. Blue Shirt's mouth was wide open as he took two slugs in his abdomen. He dropped his gun as he fell hard against the refrigerator.

Black Shirt, who had been keeping watch by the window, raised his arms. One of the policemen, who had entered through the front door, frisked him and removed his weapon.

Sylvia, who by now had found her gun under the couch just where she had hid it, put it away.

Debbie ran to Dan, and he wrapped his arms around her.

Anthony hugged Sylvia and then checked Pam's condition.

Bronson thought about his Carol—how she could have easily become a widow today. One of the police called for a paramedic as he knelt down next to Bronson. Debbie and Dan ran into the kitchen with Sylvia and Anthony close behind.

"Oh, my God!" Debbie screamed seeing Bronson drenched in blood.

"I'm okay," Bronson said as he struggled to his feet. "Just a few shards of glass. No bullets, luckily."

Debbie examined Bronson's battered face. "Jesus. You're lucky one of those didn't get you in the eye. You'd be blind as a bat."

"Yeah, it was my lucky day, I guess," Bronson said shakily.

Debbie took Bronson by the arm. "Let's go sit down until the paramedics get here."

"Yes, ma'am. Whatever you say."

"Can I get you anything?" Dan asked.

"Nah. . . . We'll . . . actually a cup of coffee would hit the spot."

Dan and Debbie burst out laughing.

"Yeah, you're okay," Dan said.

"That was very smart of you to use the code Billy and Joe to alert the officers that we were in danger," Sylvia said.

Anthony smiled. "I can't take the credit for that. It's our captain who came up with the Billy and Joe idea. I was just following orders."

"Still, I'm proud of you." She kissed him.

The paramedics arrived and tended to Bronson. He looked like the victim of a rabid woodpecker when they were through with him. Sylvia suggested he not look in the mirror. As they got up to leave Bronson cleared his throat.

Anthony and Sylvia turned to look at him.

"I realize that we're all headin' for the police station, but Anthony, I want you to ride with me." Bronson turned and joined Dan and Debbie who was gently talking to Pam.

Debbie squeezed Pam's hand. "Hold on, gal. You'll be okay. The ambulance will be here any minute now."

Bronson patted Debbie's shoulder. "Don't you worry, ma'am. She'll make it."

The sound of an approaching siren caused them all to turn to look at the front door. The paramedics came in, placed Pam on the stretcher, and carried her to the ambulance.

Once they had left, Bronson said, "We best be headin' to the police station." He turned to see if Anthony was following him.

When Anthony realized that Bronson was waiting for him, he headed his way. They drove the first block in silence. Finally, Anthony gave in. "What gives?"

"You knew I'd be checking the bugging device, so you made sure I heard your comment about Ralph Simpson. Why is that?"

Anthony looked down. "I was afraid you'd do something that would blow my cover. I'm sorry. I had no choice."

"We always have choices."

"My choice was lie to you or compromise our situation."

"What situation?"

Anthony looked out the window. He was quiet. He sighed and turned to Bronson. "I suppose my position has already been compromised, so there's no harm in telling you now."

"I'm listenin'."

"I've been working undercover. My assignment was to let them know I was on the take, and I reported to Ralph Simpson who was also supposed to be on the take."

"But he's not."

"No."

"And the purpose of all of this is—"

"Mike Patterson—the leader of the group back there—"

"That's the guy wearin' the Sedona emblem shirt?"

"Him. He's pretty big fish, but he's not, by far the biggest fish. He thinks I'm crooked, so he trusts me. I feed him information we want him to have. Sometimes it's the right information." He stole a glance at Bronson. His features had not changed and Anthony wished he knew what Bronson was thinking. "Back there at the house, I suspected Patterson knew Sylvia carried a concealed weapon, but she'd been frisked and the weapon was nowhere to be found. So I told him where it was. Other times, I make up information to fit the circumstances. He takes that knowledge and reports to his boss. He's the one we want."

"And who would that be?"

"Prickett."

"And all of this, you can prove."

Anthony's felt his features tighten. He had been expecting the question, but had hoped Bronson would have taken him at his word. "Of course."

Bronson remained quiet, staring ahead. "So now that your cover is blown, what are you goin' to do?"

Anthony shook his head and looked away.

Chapter 59

Although Mike Patterson had been alone in the interrogation room for over an hour, he showed no signs of distress. Bronson and Simpson watched him through a one-way mirror.

Simpson shook his head. "He shows no signs of wearing down, and we can't keep him there forever."

"Nope, I guess you can't."

"Maybe you and I can break him."

"You're allowin' me to go in there?"

"Sure, why not? I hear you're an ace detective. I want to see you trot your stuff."

"I can do that."

"Good."

"Okay to go in, even if I have no jurisdiction?"

"Don't see why not. You're just observing."

"But he doesn't know that."

"Right." He stood up. "We got to break Patterson before those damn DA assholes show up. They'll want to handle this, and then we're screwed."

"Yep, I know what you mean." Bronson followed him out to the hallway.

The interrogation room, a small area at the end of the hallway, seemed to Bronson to be a typical non-descript room. The white walls had no decorations, except for the one-way mirror that provided a view of the adjacent room. Four plain wooden chairs around a shabby wooden table made up the entire contents of the room. The sign on the wall read "No Smoking Allowed."

When Bronson and Simpson entered the room, Patterson didn't bother to look at them. He kept his gaze focused ahead of him. Simpson sat facing Patterson. Bronson went to the far end of the room and leaned against the wall.

"It's Mike Patterson, correct?" Simpson gave him time to acknowledge the question. When he didn't, he continued, "I'm Ralph Simpson."

A fast, almost imperceptible twitch crossed Patterson's face. Bronson noticed it, but ignored it.

"You got anything to say?" Simpson asked.

Patterson looked at Simpson for the first time. "Yeah. Aren't my rights being violated? Shouldn't I have my lawyer present?"

"Do you feel you need a lawyer?" Simpson leaned back in the chair, placed his feet on the table, and crossed his arms behind his neck.

"Seeing as how I'm innocent, I know you can't have anything on me. But that doesn't change things. Having my lawyer present is my right."

"I'm assuming that sleaze-bag Edward Wilkinson is your lawyer."

"Was that a lucky guess?"

"No, it was an educated guess." Simpson stood up. "He makes his millions defending scum like you. I'll go call him." He walked out.

For more than a minute, Bronson remained quiet. He slowly walked toward the prisoner and smiled. "You remember me?"

Patterson nodded. "You're the asshole who burst through the back door."

"That's me."

Patterson smirked.

"What puzzles me is how you can claim we have nothin' on you. We caught you red-handed."

Again, the same small twitch crossed Patterson's face.

"Oh, I see." Bronson sat on the table facing Patterson. "You think you've got it made because Simpson and Anthony are on Prickett's payroll. You think their testimony will clear you."

"I don't know what you're talking about." He smiled.

"Then let me fill you in. This is what we call a double-take. You think Simpson and Anthony are workin' for Prickett, but they're not. They're really workin' undercover for us." Bronson smiled.

Patterson continued to stare across the room, but Bronson didn't fail to notice that Patterson's eyes widened and the nerve in his face twitched.

Bronson leaned closer to the prisoner. "The way I see it, my friend, is that you're facin' the death penalty. At the very least, life in prison. It doesn't have to be that way, you know. We'll be happy to fry you, but we'd be much happier to fry Prickett. We know you have enough information on him to last three lifetimes. It's Prickett or you. It's that simple. Think about it." Bronson walked back and stood against the wall. "Your choice, my friend."

"Yeah, I get to choose my executioner—the state or Prickett."

"You'll be protected in the pen."

"Yeah, right."

"Okay, I'll talk to the DA. If you can provide him with enough inside info to put Prickett away, then maybe, you know, maybe he'll get you into the witness protection program or something like that."

Patterson's eyes lit up. "Now I'm listening."

The door opened and Simpson walked in. Patterson flashed him an evil look.

"Lawyer's on the way," Simpson said.

Bronson nodded to Simpson. "He wants to deal?"

"Really? Should I call the DA?"

Bronson looked at Patterson.

Bronson shrugged. "Not yet. Let him write it all down first. We gotta make sure it's good enough for the DA to want to cut a deal."

"Oh, don't worry," Patterson said. "It'll be plenty good enough."

"We'll see. I'll get a pad," Simpson said.

Simpson left the room for a minute and returned with a pad of paper and a pen. He shoved it in front of Patterson.

"I'd rather see you fry myself," Simpson said as he glared at Patterson.

Bronson took Simpson's arm and pulled him toward the door. "Come on. It's better this way."

They left the room to give Patterson time to work on his confession. Once outside a wide smiled came over Simpson's face.

"You *are* good, Bronson. Witness protection—that's a good one. Let me buy you cup of coffee."

"Sure thing. Just what I need after a hard day's work."

Chapter 60

Bronson looked over Dan's shoulder and read the article on Dan's monitor.

"So what do you think?" Dan asked Bronson once he had finished reading the article Dan had written about Prickett.

"Sounds good."

Dan leaned back in his chair and felt a delightful rush of excitement at having successfully completed this task. "We nailed him. We actually nailed the bastard!"

"Looks like it." Bronson pointed to the monitor. "Where are you going with this?"

"I've already contacted the local paper. The news editor is waiting for this story. She tells me that it'll be tomorrow's headlines." Dan reread the article one last time. "Guess I'm ready to send it." Dan moved the cursor to the send sign and clicked. "It's gone."

"Just like that."

Dan nodded. "Modern technology. You gotta love it."

"Yep, it's nice. Real nice. But what's nicer is that this is exactly what Barbara Bloomer wanted—and you met her deadline."

"Won't wonders ever cease?" Dan picked up his cell phone, clipped it to his belt, and stood. "I believe Barbara is waiting for me. Want to come?"

"Thought you'd never ask."

* * *

"I missed your guard at the gate." Dan leaned back on the couch. He and Bronson sat in Barbara's library. Floor to ceiling bookshelves occupied facing walls. Glass sliding doors led to an atrium filled with lush, green plants and an array of various shades of flowers. Soft classical music filled the air.

Dan felt that instead of being in Las Vegas, he was somewhere in the Caribbean. "So where is your guard?"

"My father lived one type of life. I chose a different route. My life doesn't require the use of bodyguards or gatekeepers. My father's did."

"I think you made the right decision, ma'am. That gatekeeper was bad news."

"He wasn't very happy when I let him go, but I guess that's how it goes." Barbara sat back in the recliner and folded her leg under her lap. "But enough about my gatekeeper. I'm sure neither of you came over here to talk about him."

"You're right about that, ma'am."

"Could you possibly be here to tell me that you've met my deadline, and that you've finished that exposé on Prickett?"

Dan opened the folder he had been carrying, retrieved the papers, and handed them to Barbara. "That's exactly what we came to tell you." He pointed to the papers he had given to her. "That's it, right there. I printed a copy for you. It will be tomorrow's lead story." An arrow of remorse buried itself deep in Dan's gut. He was glad to know that he had a hand in sending Prickett to prison. But how would Young Greg feel about it? Before the day was over, he'd have to confront Young Greg, and let him know that he was the one responsible for his father's arrest.

The door opened and Erica, pushing a roll-along cart, entered. The cart contained matching crème and sugar bowls, a large china plate filled with an arrangement of cookies, and candy dishes filled with chocolates and a variety of hard candies.

Erica poured Bronson and Barbara each a cup of coffee, then she handed Dan a tall glass of homemade lemonade.

"Thank you, Erica. Did you bring the recipe?"

"I did." She reached for the bottom shelf and retrieved a folded piece of paper. She handed it to Barbara.

"Thank you. You may leave."

Erica nodded once and walked out.

Barbara handed Bronson the folded piece of paper. "As I recall, you wanted the coffee recipe. I had Erica write it down for you."

"This is wonderful. Maybe now my Carol will be able to make a decent cup of coffee. She's a wonderful woman, but she can't do coffee worth beans. No pun intended. I don't know what she puts in it but it is terribly bitter." He looked at the recipe. "Thank you, ma'am, and please, thank Erica for me."

Barbara nodded and pointed to the cart. "Please, help yourselves."

Bronson pocketed a handful of hard candies, then busied himself fixing his coffee. Dan chose three different kinds of cookies, a chocolate wafer and two that seemed to be either lemon or sugar cookies. He ate more to calm his nerves than to feed his hunger.

Barbara ignored her coffee and read the article. When she finished, she placed the pages neatly on her lap and looked up. "So this will appear in tomorrow's paper?"

Dan bit into the cookie. Lemon. He loved lemon. "Guaranteed to be there. In fact, I've been assured it will be tomorrow's front page headline."

"You absolutely sure?"

"Yes, it's a done deal."

"And everything in the article is true?"

"Of course. I wouldn't have put it there if it hadn't been properly verified. I can prove every word in the article. Prickett is going down without a doubt." He picked up two more lemon cookies.

Barbara smiled, poured some cream into her coffee, and stirred it. "Technically, I should wait until tomorrow to verify that the article will be there. But, Mr. Springer, I have found you to be a man of your word. I believe I can trust you."

"You can."

Barbara flashed him a weak smile and looked away. Bronson sat up and gave Barbara a hard look.

"I was wonderin' ma'am, could you clear up a small detail for me." Bronson retrieved his notebook and thumbed through it. "Ah, here it is. When Dan and Marcos rescued Young Greg, Dan told me he was worried that they were takin' too long, and you'd go upstairs and catch them. Is that right?"

Dan was about to bite into his cookie. Instead he set it down and nodded.

Bronson looked at Barbara. "Mind tellin' me why you never went upstairs to see what was goin' on?"

Barbara attempted a smile. "Didn't Dan tell you I can't stand the sight of blood?"

"Ah, the blood. Yes. He mentioned it."

"Then?"

"Now that's not the real reason is it, ma'am?"

Barbara folded her arms.

Dan studied her, then cast his gaze on Bronson. "What exactly is it you're trying to say?"

"That Barbara is your informer."

Barbara looked down.

Dan looked up.

Barbara looked into Dan's questioning eyes and finally nodded.

"You set up your own father?"

Tears welled in Barbara's eyes. "I didn't. . .it wasn't supposed. . ." She stood up and wiped the tears away. She moved toward the window, giving Bronson and Dan her back. She stood silent except for the occasional sob that shook her body.

Bronson leaned back on the couch and sipped his coffee. After a long pause, he said, "You did the right thing, ma'am."

"Knowing that doesn't make it any easier."

"Sometimes doin' the right thing is not exactly the choice we'd want to make."

"I don't understand why you did it," Dan said.

Slowly, Barbara turned to face him. "I told you before. My father chose one kind of life. I chose another. I couldn't stand to see him harm an innocent seventeen-year-old boy."

"So you used me to rescue Young Greg."

Barbara nodded.

Bronson set his cup down and grabbed a lemon cookie. "Thing I find interestin' is hearin' why out of all the people in the world, you chose Dan."

"I knew he had lost his little girl. I figured he'd welcome the opportunity to save Young Greg."

"Why not just go to the police?" Bronson poured himself another cup of coffee.

"Seemed too cruel. My father would know I had betrayed him. I couldn't stand that. I figured that with Dan rescuing him, my father would never know I was the one behind the scheme."

"But you must have realized what would happen when Prickett found out who kidnapped his son," Dan said.

"I was sure my father could protect himself. I mean, he had to figure Prickett would eventually find out who had taken his son. I really thought he'd be okay." Barbara crossed her arms. "Do you know what it's like to live with yourself day in and day out and know that you betrayed your own father?"

Dan stood up and walked over to her. They stared at each other for a long time. He wrapped his arms around her and she let her head rest on his shoulder.

After a while, Dan said, "You don't know anything about Diana, do you?"

Barbara's features filled with sorrow and regret. She shook her head and looked away.

"But I do," Bronson said.

Chapter 61

"We will soon know the answer." Bronson waved the thick stack of notes he had made on Dan's case. "The answer is buried somewhere here. We've just got to find it. Why don't we hold another brainstormin' session? I know we'll come up with the answer. Guaranteed."

A wave of despair numbed Dan's senses. What was the use? All they were doing was wandering around aimlessly—groping for answers. They were like blind men in a maze. "Will that really accomplish anything?"

"It's worth a try."

Was it really? "I've been searching for Diana for almost seven years, and I'm not any closer to finding her now than I was then."

"Exactly my point. You've been at it for seven years. How could one more day hurt?"

Dan slowly nodded. He would spend the rest of his life searching for her if he needed to. "We'll meet in my apartment in an hour."

* * *

Debbie, Sylvia, and Anthony all arrived at the same time. Dan kissed Debbie, hugged Sylvia, and shook Anthony's hand. "Are you two still sticking around Debbie?"

Sylvia smiled. "She's never really too far from our sight, but we're returning to work."

"I appreciate all you've done for her."

"Me, too!" Debbie said and everyone laughed.

The doorbell rang.

"That's got to be Bronson." Dan opened the door and was surprised to see Barbara was with him.

Introductions were made and beers were opened for all except Bronson. He preferred coffee, but not wanting to offend anyone, he poured a touch of rum into his coffee. They sat around Dan's dinette sipping their drinks.

"I suggested meetin' because I know we're this close to findin' Diana." Bronson squeezed his thumb and index finger together. "Thought maybe if we all put our heads together, we're bound to come up with some strong leads. So, who wants to start?"

"I do," said Sylvia. "I suggest we begin by listing what we know and what that could mean."

"We know that Dan has seen a picture of a three or four-year-old girl whom he believes is his daughter," Anthony said.

"And what can we conclude from this?" Bronson asked.

"She's alive and well." Dan realized this wasn't necessarily true, so he added, "Or at least she was at the time of the picture."

Debbie reached out and squeezed his hand.

"True, true." Bronson sipped his coffee. "What else?"

Silence filled the air as everyone considered the question. Sylvia's face lit up. "Since Derek had a picture of her, that means that either a) Derek was the kidnapper or b) he knew the kidnapper."

"What we don't know," Anthony said, "is whether the kidnapper is the one who actually has Diana, or if he/she did it for money."

"Good. Let's pursue that angle." Bronson turned to Barbara who sat bolt upright, her hands resting on her lap. She hadn't touched her beer. "This is where you come in, ma'am."

A startled look crossed her face, and she pointed to herself. "Me? I don't know anything about this."

"Sure you do. All I want you to do is tell us once again why Prickett didn't go after you when he found out that your father was responsible for kidnaping Young Greg."

Barbara wet her lips. When she spoke, her voice sounded small and timid. "It doesn't work that way."

"Ah. You care to explain why?"

"Because of the code of honor."

"Which means?"

"Detective Bronson, I have explained this over and over again."

"Humor me, please. One more time."

"The code of honor says that you always go for the person responsible, not his family."

"And your father—he followed this code?"

"Of course."

"Then why would he break it by goin' for Prickett's kid?"

"Because. . .because. . ." Barbara looked around the room as though the answer perched in the room's hidden corners. A dull, glaze covered her eyes, and she focused her attention on Dan. "Because. . .he knew. . .Prickett had broken . . . the code of honor first." Her eyes glistened and she wiped her eyes.

"Meanin'?"

"Meaning Prickett had gone after someone's family."

"And you know this because. . ."

Barbara closed her eyes and a small tremble shook her body. "Cosmo Grajeda—you remember him as the giant who held Young Greg prisoner."

Dan nodded. The image of that giant touching his wife, his child, made his blood boil.

Barbara continued, "Several months ago, he got drunk and he, uh, came on to me." A look of disgust filled her face as the memory returned to her. "I. . .I suppose he was trying to impress me by telling me how tough he was. He started by telling me about how he. . ." She glanced toward Dan's direction then quickly looked away.

Dan's gaze was focused on Barbara. He couldn't believe where this story was going.

Barbara reached for her beer, stared at it for a long time, then took a large gulp. "Cosmo described in gruesome detail how he had beat up this woman. She. . .she dragged herself down the hallway. . .and. . .and he'd. . .he'ddd. . .kick her just to hear her scream." Tears streamed down her face. "I. . . I couldn't stand to hear any more so I ran out."

Thick silence filled the air. Dan stared at Barbara.

Barbara brought her hands to her face as she quietly sobbed. She wiped away her tears, then raised her head. "As I ran out, he laughed and said, 'Don't you want to hear about the baby?'"

Chapter 62

Tears of anger and resentment clouded Barbara's vision as she ran down the hallway. Cosmo's mocking laughter echoed in her mind.

She reached the safety of her bedroom. She slammed the door shut behind her and leaned against the door. Her body shook as the images formed in her mind.

Cosmo beating the woman.

The woman, folded over in pain on the floor.

Cosmo kicking her.

Over and over.

Had her father ordered this? Had he been the first to violate the code of honor? Would families from now on be game for anyone's revenge? Was *she* in danger?

Barbara threw herself on the bed. "Oh Dad, why? Why?" She sat up and wiped her tears. She took in several deliberate long breaths. Slowly, she started to calm down.

She walked over to the sink, splashed some water on her face and ran a brush through her hair. She knew her father wasn't home, but Cosmo would tell her all she needed to know.

She found him where she had expected him to be. In her living room by the bar fixing himself another drink.

When she walked in, he smiled, a curvature of the lips that seemed more like a leer. "What's the matter, Sweet Cheeks, did you come to hear more?"

"I want to know if my dad ordered you to do that."

"Actually, no."

"Then who?"

Cosmo squinted as though considering if he should tell her. "What the hell, right? It was Prickett."

"But my dad knew?"

"Of course he knew. He works for Prickett, but I work

for your old man. I don't do nothing unless your dad tells me it's okay."

Barbara had nodded and walked out.

* * *

"That day, I decided I'd never live a life like my father's." Barbara paused, shook her head, and looked down. "I'm sorry, Dan, I didn't tell you this before."

Sometime during Barbara's narrative, Dan had stood up, walked over to the window, and stood with his arms folded over his chest, looking out the window.

Debbie went to him and tried to hug him. He shook his head and gently pushed her away. Debbie leaned against the kitchen counter and stood close to Dan.

"Why didn't you mention it before?" As Dan spoke, he slowly turned to face Barbara.

"As silly as it sounds, I was trying to protect my father. Maybe he didn't order it, but he approved it by letting Cosmo do the...deed." She looked up toward the ceiling and her lips trembled.

"And you knew this all along?" Bronson asked.

Barbara dropped her shoulders as her face paled and froze. The question appeared to have turned her face to stone.

"I'd advise you, ma'am, to get yourself a good lawyer. You're an accessory to a kidnappin' and possible murder. I'll have to make a report."

Barbara nodded. "I understand."

Dan threw his arms up in the air.

"So that's it? We're no further ahead than we were before." He rubbed his hand over his face.

"Ah, but you're wrong."

Everyone's attention turned to Bronson. He continued, "We know Prickett's behind it. Not only do we have Barbara's testimony, we have the logic behind it, and that may lead us to the cause."

Sylvia's forehead furrowed. "What do you mean?"

"We know why Elko Bloomer broke the code of honor when he took Prickett's kid. Way I see it is Elko wanted more power. So he sets up some deals on the side. He's laundering money, but he's worried Prickett will find out. So how do you keep Prickett's mind busy? You take his son. But Elko's a smart man. He knows what will happen to the man responsible for kidnapin' his son. So he finds a guinea pig and has him killed. He tells Prickett who did it. Prickett is impressed. Elko moves up the ladder and is richer." He moved closer to Barbara. His gaze pierced hers. "Am I right, ma'am?"

Without looking at Bronson, Barbara nodded.

Bronson leaned back in his chair. "So Elko had somethin' to gain so he broke the code of honor. And that accordin' to him was okay because Prickett had broken it first when he had somethin' to gain."

Dan walked back to the table and sat on the empty chair next to Bronson. "You're talking about the drug story. Are you suggesting that Prickett was also dealing with drugs? If that is so, then if I killed the series, that would benefit him."

"That's a possibility."

Dan studied Bronson. "But not a likely one." When Bronson didn't answer, Dan said, "Call me dense, but what exactly is the point you're trying to make?"

"I just have a feelin' that the drug business was just a cover-up."

"A cover-up for what?" Sylvia asked.

"Ah, that's the million dollar question. What did Prickett have to benefit?" Bronson took out his notes and read them. "Ah, here it is." He turned to Dan. "Somethin' you said bothers me."

Dan felt his heart race. "What's that?"

"About the third time I had you retell me the story, you mentioned a detail you had left out before."

"And that is?"

"You said that you and Young Greg talked about his brother who lives in Tucson."

"I believe I mentioned that, yes."

"And do you remember what you said brought on that conversation?"

"Not offhand."

"You said that Young Greg told you that you remind him of his brother."

"That's right. But what does that have to do—wait a minute, you're not saying that Young Greg's brother has my daughter?"

"He could."

"Impossible."

"Why?"

"Young Greg told me he has a nephew, not a niece."

"Maybe he's mistakin' or lyin'. Take your pick." Bronson paused to review his notes. "Follow me in my line of thinkin'. Prickett sees you and your lovely wife somewhere. The mall, maybe. He sees Linda is close to delivery. You resemble his son. Maybe even Linda resembles his daughter-in-law. This could be his grandchild. Young Greg's brother—Brad, isn't it?—he wants a kid. His wife is sterile or maybe he is. Either way, no baby for them. They try adoption. Everyone knows he's part of the Las Vegas Mafia. That's no way to bring up a kid. He's refused adoption, or his name gets put at the very bottom of the list and stays there. So Prickett does good for his son. He has you followed. Does his homework. He finds out you're writin' an exposé on Las Vegas drugs. Perfect opportunity. The idea is born."

"If you're right, then that means that Young Greg deliberately lied to me even after I rescued him." Dan looked up at Debbie. "I still have his cell number. How about I call him and tell him I'm taking you to meet him?"

Debbie nodded.

Chapter 63

Young Greg agreed to meet Dan and Debbie at the McDonald's on Las Vegas Boulevard. Dan ordered a Sprite for himself and a diet Coke for Debbie.

Debbie and Dan took their sodas and joined Young Greg at a booth. He had ordered a soda and French fries. His eyes lit up when he saw Debbie. "Ms. Gunther, it's. . .I'm Greg Prickett. They call me Young Greg, but I'm not really young at all."

Debbie smiled and scooted into the booth. Dan slid next to her. "Dan's told me a lot about you. I'm glad I finally got to meet you."

Young Greg smiled. "I got some friends who'd love to meet you. Would you mind if I call them?" He reached for his cell phone.

"Not right now." Dan put a straw in his drink. "This is more of a business call."

Young Greg sat up straight. "Is this about my dad?"

Dan nodded. "Mostly."

Young Greg pushed his soda away. "He was arrested today. You knew that, didn't you?"

Dan nodded. "Yes, I know. Tomorrow's leading article will reveal a lot of terrible details that will probably send him to the electric chair."

Young Greg's features tightened. "How do you know that?" He looked at Dan.

Dan looked away.

"Oh, I see. You wrote the article."

Dan nodded. "And I wanted you to hear it from me before you read tomorrow's headlines."

Young Greg stared at his food and was quiet for a long time. "It's not your fault, man. My dad brought this on himself." He took a fry, dipped it in the ketchup, looked at it, and set it back down. "Thanks for telling me."

"I'm sorry."

"Don't be. I'm graduating in a couple of weeks. Then I'm out of here."

"Will you join your brother in Tucson?"

"Maybe."

"I think that would be a good idea," Debbie said. "Dan tells me he's made a good life for himself over there."

"Yeah, away from the family name. He changed his name. No one knows about his Vegas connections."

"What's his new name?"

Young Greg shrugged. "Don't know. Dad made sure I wouldn't find out. He figured that the less ties my brother has to Vegas, the better off he'd be, so he didn't want me bothering him. Besides, Dad always assumed I'd be the one to take over the family business."

"But that's not what you plan to do?" Dan leaned forward.

Young Greg shook his head. "I want to find my brother and do like he did. I want to break all ties with Vegas and start fresh. Do you think you could help me find my brother? I have no idea how to go about doing something like that."

Dan leaned back and inwardly smiled.

Debbie dabbed her lips with a napkin. "We'll find him for you. We know that he lives in Tucson and that he manages a snowbird community. What else can you tell us about him?"

"He's ten years older than me. That would make him twenty-eight." His looked around the room, as though trying to think what else he knew. "That's it, I guess. That's all I know. My parents don't even know I know that much. I overheard them talking. That's how I found out that he lives and works in Tucson, and that he changed his name."

Dan took a small sip of his soda and set the cup down. "That'll give us a place to begin. If need be, we'll drive down to Tucson." Dan thought of his lunch date with his cousin Ivy. He made a mental note to call her and change the day. "It must be very hard on your mother, not seeing her own son and not playing with her own granddaughter."

Young Greg smirked. "I guess. I never thought about that."

Dan nodded and looked at Debbie. He noticed that Young Greg hadn't bothered to correct him about the child's gender.

Chapter 64

The phone rang four times before a cheerful voice at the other end answered, "Good morning. How can I help you?"

Dan looked at the half page ad in the Tucson's yellow pages. He had called this campground first because of the size of the ad. He figured Young Greg's brother wouldn't be lacking for money. "Is this the Happy Trails Campground?"

"Sure is."

Of course it was. Her cheery tone told him so. "I need to get in touch with my sister who's staying at one of the campgrounds in Tucson."

"Oh, dear. There are a lot of campgrounds here in Tucson. Our weather attracts a lot of people trying to escape the cold winters. I can check our roster and see if she's here. What's her name?"

"Debbie Springer."

When Debbie heard her first name mentioned along with Dan's last name, she looked at Dan and glared.

Dan smiled and threw her a kiss.

"Springer?" the lady over the phone asked. "That doesn't ring any bells." There was a pause, and Dan could hear the turning of pages. "No, sorry. No Springers. I do have a Debbie but with a different last name. I'm sorry I couldn't be of help."

"Maybe you still can help me."

"How's that?"

"Debbie told me about the campground owners. She said they were a young couple in their late twenties. They have a little girl, almost seven."

"I know exactly who you're talking about."

Dan gave Debbie the thumbs-up symbol. "Great. Who's that?"

"The Albrights, Bob and Heather. They own the Sunny Dale's Campground. Do you want their phone number?"

"That would be great." Dan wrote down the number, thanked her for her help, and replaced the phone on its cradle. He waved the paper with the information in front of him. "I got it. I think. I hope. Oh, Debbie, you don't know how it feels to know that I might finally hold my little girl in my arms." At this moment, the sky and all its stars belonged to him.

Dan sat on the bed in the motel room. An opened telephone book rested by him. The rest of the bed was scattered with city maps and pamphlets advertising various campgrounds.

Debbie leaned against the dresser. "Are we going to call them?"

"Only to get directions. Then we're going to see them."

"Then what?"

The question felt like an arrow stabbing his heart. "What do you mean, then what? If it's them—and I'm positive it is—then, I finally get to pick up my daughter."

"Just like that?"

A painful confusion ripped at him. Why wasn't she happy for him? Was she jealous? Is that what all of this was about? He chose not to answer. He gave her a look that he hoped clearly meant that she needed to explain herself.

"Dan, Diana doesn't know you."

"I realize that."

"What if she's happy with the people she calls Mom and Dad? Are you willing to destroy her happiness?"

"Damn it, Debbie." Dan stood up without bothering to move the phone that had been resting on his lap. It landed on the floor with a loud thud. He headed for the bathroom. "Don't spoil this for me." He slammed the door behind him.

Debbie stood with her hands in her lap looking down at the carpet and listening to the telephone's disconnected dial tone.

Chapter 65

Sunny Dale's Campground was located on the west side of town. Each unit contained its own paved carport and small private yard. The sign at the entryway read All Visitors Must Report to the Main Office. An arrow showed the office's location. It was situated next to the large pool and shuffleboard court.

Dan parked in one of the two empty visitors' parking spaces. He wet his lips and wiped his face with his opened hand. "I'm ready. Let's do this."

Debbie frowned. "Dan—"

He waved his hand. "If you'd rather wait in the car, I'll understand."

Debbie shook her head. "I'll go with you."

Together, hand-in-hand, Dan and Debbie headed toward the office. Dan saw his hand shake as he reached for the door and swung it open. He stuck his head in and saw that the room was empty. "Hello?"

A male voice from the backroom said, "Be there in a minute."

Dan and Debbie stepped inside and Dan closed the door behind them. He took the opportunity to look around. When he reached the counter, he saw a picture frame facing away from him. He turned it around so he could look at it. "Oh, God." Dan felt the blood leave his face. He turned to Debbie. "It's her."

"May I help you?"

Dan turned. He immediately recognized Brad/Bob. The resemblance between him and his brother was undeniable. His very pregnant wife stood beside him.

Bob looked at Dan's hands and back up at him.

Dan returned the picture to its place. "That's a beautiful child."

"It's my daughter, Penny."

"Penny Albright." Dan whispered the name as though he tested its sound.

Bob squinted and his smile faded. "Do I know you?" He wrapped his arm around his wife.

"You know of me."

Bob looked at his daughter's picture then up at Dan. A spark of recognition crossed his eyes. "Oh, God, no," he whispered.

"We need to talk."

Bob nodded.

Heather leaned closer to her husband. "Who are these people?"

Bob shook his head. "In a minute, honey, I'll explain. Right now let's page Sandie and tell her to come watch the front office."

Heather's forehead creased. She did as she was told.

While they waited for Sandie to show up, Dan reached out for Debbie. "I'm Dan Springer and this is Debbie Gunther."

The look in Heather's face reminded Dan of a child who had just received an unexpected gift. "The singer?"

Debbie nodded.

The front door opened and a tall, skinny woman in her early twenties stepped in. She wore very tight shorts. "What's up?"

"We need you to watch the counter," Heather said. "Bob and I will be talking to these folks in the back room. Make sure we're not disturbed."

"Sure." She gave Dan and Debbie a curious look. She stared at Debbie as though she recognized her, started to say something, but changed her mind. She headed toward the counter.

Bob and Heather led Dan and Debbie down a hallway and to their left.

Chapter 66

The back room served as a crowded office. Two side-by-side metal cabinets, a wooden desk, and four metal, folding chairs with cushioned seats made up the entire contents.

"Make yourselves comfortable," Bob pointed at the chairs.

Dan and Debbie sat down.

"You know who I am."

"I have an idea."

Heather turned to her husband. "Will somebody tell me what's going on?"

Bob wrapped his arm around her. "They're here about Penny."

"Penny? What about. . ." Her eyes grew as big as saucers. She covered her mouth. "No. No. She's my baby. Please don't."

Dan swallowed hard. He kept his gaze fixed in front of him.

Heather stood up and began to pace in the small area. "Your father promised. . . he said we'd never. . . Can't you call your father?"

"Won't do any good," Dan said. "He's been arrested."

Bob closed his eyes and Heather broke out in tears.

Bob turned to Dan, his eyes filled with bitterness. "Just exactly what is it that you want, Mr. Springer?"

Dan took a deep breath trying to control his emotions. He looked at Heather's tear streaked face. "Is. . .Diana happy?"

"*Penny* is a happy child. We've surrounded her with love. We've taught her manners, respect for others, and she's well adjusted. It wouldn't be right to destroy the only life she's known."

Debbie leaned forward. "Mr. Albright, you speak with anger and resentment as though this was Dan's fault. Remember, he is the victim. What your father did—"

"Wait. What are you talking about? Just exactly what did my father do?"

"How did he explain the baby to you?" Dan asked.

"He told me that you were an abusive husband and a drunk. The mother was petrified that you would harm the baby and that's why she gave her away."

Dan looked at him. "If you believed that, then why did you change your name?"

"Dad said it'd be best. You might come looking for us. He said you were a violent man."

"Do you really believe that?"

Bob leaned back on his chair and let out a long-drawn sigh. "Now that I've met you, no. You seem neither violent nor a drunk." He closed his eyes and massaged them. "I should have known better than to believe my father. How did he get hold of the baby?"

Debbie walked over and stood next to Heather, and put her arm around her. "Are you sure you're up to hearing this? It's not a very nice story."

Heather nodded. "I need to know."

"In that case, why don't you sit down?"

Dan waited until Heather had settled in next to her husband. Dan looked up at Debbie, his eyes telling her he couldn't go through this again.

Debbie stood beside him and put her hand on his shoulder. "They need to know."

Dan nodded. He wet his lips and told the story one more time. His voice broke several times, and he had to pause before he could continue. Long after Dan finished, no one spoke. Heather's body shook with sobs. Bob sat with his back arched, head down, and his hands tightly clasped between his knees.

Even Debbie, who had heard the story several times, found herself crying softly.

"I'm sorry." Bob cleared his throat. "I had no idea."

"Wh-what's g-going to h-happen?" Heather spoke between sobs. "Are you g-going to t-take P-Penny away?"

Debbie felt Dan's body tense.

A long minute dragged by.

"No."

Debbie looked at the man she loved and her heart swelled with pride. If anyone ever deserved a hero's medal, it was Dan.

"It would tear her apart, wouldn't it?" Dan's voice came out as a hushed whisper.

"Yes."

Heather stood up, bent down, and gave Dan a kiss on the cheek. "Thank you. I have no words to express—"

Dan raised his hand to stop her. "I'm doing this for Diana. . .uh. . .Penny. But when she's an adult, I want to tell her the truth."

Both Heather and Bob nodded. Bob reached out for his wife's hand and said, "I'd like to suggest that we draw some legal papers stating that we maintain legal custody, but of course, we will consult you on all matters."

Dan looked down at the floor. He didn't move. He didn't even breathe. Time stretched to eternity. Slowly, he nodded.

"Would you like to meet her?" Heather asked.

Dan shot to his feet. "No."

He walked out.

Chapter 67

Debbie sat in a puzzled stupor and stared at the empty chair that Dan had occupied. "Excuse me," she said. "We'll be back in a minute." She ran after Dan.

By the time she caught up with him, he was already sliding behind the wheel. She walked over to the driver's side and stared at him.

"Get in."

"No."

"What?"

"I'm not getting in."

"Why not?"

"You'll drive away."

"I'll drive away anyway, with or without you, so you might as well get in."

"Dan, listen to yourself."

"Last chance. Get in." He turned on the ignition.

Debbie crossed her arms. "You! Get out of the car."

His gaze met hers.

"Now!"

He turned off the engine, stepped out of the car, leaned against it, and folded his arms.

"You've spent almost seven years looking for Diana, and now that you found her, you won't even look at her?"

He gave her a pinched smile. "That's right." His sky-blue eyes were as hard as crystal.

A wave of despair washed over Debbie. She felt as if she were standing on a narrow ledge and the earth under her feet could crumble at any second. She looked up at the angry, gray sky.

No! She would not let him do this. She had to be strong. For Dan. For herself. "Many children split their time between their parents."

"Are you suggesting that Diana spend her weekdays here with...them and weekends in Vegas with us? Because if you are—"

"We could move here, to Tucson," Debbie said.

Dan raised his eyebrows. "We? Are you saying that we should move in together?"

"Maybe. We could move to Tucson so you can be close to Diana."

"What about your job? Your career?"

"There's no job, no career. At the end of this month, Bill's letting me go."

Dan opened his mouth to say something, but nothing came out. His eyes reflected an expression of genuine astonishment. "Why?"

"I'm creating too much of a scandal, he says. It's bad for the show. It's bad for Colette's reputation." She looked down as her shoulders sagged.

Dan sighed, then opened his arms and she went into his embrace. "I'm so sorry, honey." His voice was softer, his tone, warmer. "I've been so wrapped up in finding Diana, I've neglected to see how this affected you."

She looked up at Dan. "It's fine. Really. Maybe I can open a dancing and singing school here in Tucson. I could even try the theater over here. It'll be good." She smiled at him. "What about you? Can you leave your job in Vegas?"

"For Diana? In a second. But we still haven't solved a damn thing."

Debbie pushed away from his embrace. "Meaning?"

"I will not have Diana tossed back and forth like a ball. I'm sure she's happy here and that's all I want. Her happiness."

"And you'll be miserable until she turns eighteen or twenty-one or whatever age you feel she's old enough to learn the truth."

Dan shrugged. "I can live with that as long as I know she's okay."

"But you don't have to do that."

Dan's face remained impassive, but his eyebrows knit slightly in puzzlement. "What do you have in mind?"

"Bob could introduce you as Uncle Dan. Since we'll be living here in Tucson, you can visit her as often as you want. You'll get to know each other a little at a time, and that will give her a chance to grow to love you. Then, when she'd old enough, she'll be ready to hear the truth. She won't be bounced back and forth. All we will be doing is babysitting. We can take her to the movies, the park, and maybe later on, Disneyland."

Dan placed a finger to his lip and gazed up at the sky. Debbie knew he was carefully considering her words, his thoughts focused beyond any place she could see. "Sounds like something I could go for." He cupped her head in his hands and looked deep into her eyes. He pulled her toward him and held her tightly. "This isn't quite what I had in mind. I had planned something much more romantic but for now, this will have to do."

He pulled away from the embrace and looked at her. "If we move to Tucson, or even if we don't move, I want to make you my wife."

The second their eyes met, something moved between them, like a jolt of electricity. Debbie wanted to scream *yes*, but a thought at the back of her mind stopped her from doing so. "You're right. This isn't the time to talk about marriage."

A frown formed on Dan's face. "I love you, Debbie. Don't you want to marry me?"

"More than anything else in the world. But if I accept

now, I'll always wonder if you wanted to marry me because of me, or because you wanted to provide something for Diana."

"No, sweetheart, please don't think that. I wanted to marry you even before I found Diana." He reached out and hugged her.

Debbie allowed herself to dwell in the comfort of Dan's arms. "Later, we can discuss what we want to do about us. For now, let's go see if the Albrights will go for my suggestion."

Chapter 68

Hand-in-hand, Dan and Debbie returned to the park office. Bob and Heather stood side-by-side, anxiety written on both of their faces. Heather's eyes were red.

"We have a possible solution," Dan said.

"Let's go back to the back room and talk." Heather led the way down the hall.

They occupied the same chairs they had before. Dan bit his lip, took a deep breath, and paraphrased Debbie's speech. When he finished, Dan held his breath and reached for Debbie's hand.

Bob and Heather exchanged looks. Heather nodded.

Dan let out his breath in a whoosh.

"Thank you," Bob said. "I know what a sacrifice you've just made. I wish this had never happened to you. You're truly a loving father, and I'll make sure that when Penny is old enough, she'll know what you've done for her."

Dan nodded and looked away.

"Not that I'm questioning your intent or anything like that," Bob said, "but if it's all the same to you, I'd still like to draw those legal documents, and, like I said, we will consult you on everything."

"I understand."

"One more thing," Bob said.

Silence filled the room.

"You said Young Greg would like to come here. Please tell him he is more than welcome anytime."

"I will."

Heather stood up. "In that case, are you ready to meet your daughter?"

Dan felt as if a thousand needles stabbed him. He nodded and Heather walked out.

Dan ran his fingers through his hair and straightened his shirt.

"Relax," Debbie said. "You look fine."

"What if she doesn't like me?"

"How could she not like you?"

The door opened and Heather entered. Beside her, holding on to her mother's hand, stood a not quite four-foot-tall girl with golden brown hair that came down to her shoulders. She had a slightly up-turned chin and a wide forehead.

"Penny, this is your Uncle Dan."

Dan dropped to his knees so he'd be eye level with her. "Hello, Penny."

Penny released her grasp from her mother's hand, but remained by her side.

Dan smiled. She reminded him so much of Linda. His heart swelled with love.

Slowly, Penny walked toward Dan. She stood in front of him, studying him. Her almond-shaped, light-brown eyes sparkled like tiny precious stones.

His smile widened.

She smiled back. This was Linda's smile. Dan's heart broke.

Debbie placed her hand over her mouth as she watched the interaction between Dan and his daughter.

"I didn't know I had an uncle. Where have you been?"

Dan shrugged. "Well, I live in Las Vegas. That's a long way from here."

"Mom and dad never talk about you."

"Ah, well. . . . That's why I came to visit—to see you and catch up on old times."

"Will you come to my birthday party?"

Dan looked up at Heather.

She nodded.

"I'd love to come."

"Good. I can't wait to tell everyone I have an uncle."

Dan smiled. "Hey. I noticed a swing set outside. Do you like to swing?"

Penney's eyes lit up. "Un huh. Will you push me?"

Dan nodded. "You bet."

"I like to go really, really high."

"No problem. Come on."

Dan stood up and followed his daughter out into a brighter, better world, a world that had been changed forever.

Other Titles by L.C. Hayden

Who's Susan

When Colette Died

Where Secrets Lie

When Angels Touch

For more information on L.C. Hayden

visit http://toppub.com

Or

http://lchayden.freeservers.com

Also from Top Publications

2003 Agatha Winner
Children/Young Adult

Red Card, A Zeke Armstrong Mystery

by Matthew LaBrot and Daniel Hale

Top Publications, Ltd. ISBN 1-929976-15-1

Trade Paperback $7.95 181 pages

After living in a series of far-flung countries - and finding more than his share of trouble along the way - Zeke Armstrong thought he would finally lead the life of a "normal" thirteen-year-old when he moved to Dallas and joined the Sundogs soccer team. Instead, he goes to the Lone Star Invitational tournament and soon finds himself in the middle of another adventure when someone tries to take his coach out of the game...permanently. Will Zeke solve the mystery and help his team win the playoffs, or will he be the next victim?